The Damned Society: Smoke and Mirrors

L. J. Elliott

The Damned Society

First published in 2020
by Wallace Publishing, United Kingdom
www.wallacepublishing.co.uk

All Rights Reserved
Copyright © L. J. Elliott

The right of L. J. Elliott to be identified as the author of this work has been asserted in accordance with section 77 and 78 of the Copyright Designs and Patents Act 1988.

This book is sold under condition that it shall not, by way of trade or otherwise, be lent, re-sold, hired out or otherwise circulated in any form of binding or cover other than that in which it is published and without a similar condition including this condition being imposed on the subsequent purchaser.

This is a work of fiction. Names, characters, businesses, places, events and incidents are either the products of the author's imagination or used in a fictitious manner. Any resemblance to actual persons, living or dead, or actual events is purely coincidental.

Typesetting courtesy of Wallace Author Services, United Kingdom
www.wallaceauthorservices.weebly.com

Cover design courtesy of KGHH Publishing, United Kingdom
www.kensingtongorepublishing.com

Dedication

*To my family. The music that inspires me.
And my sister, Francesca.*

Prologue

The smoke built around me with speed, carrying a taste of destruction as it vaped through my senses. The air gushed past my skin, getting heavier in pace with each breath I took. The smell of burnt paper lingering as it flowed around in the destructive zone that I was creating. I had never lost control like this before, yet at the same time, had never felt so happy about it.

My mind was not instantly filled with regret or sadness at the fact I had let my power control me. In fact, it was quite the opposite. I was glad because it was the thing that ultimately helped me out in the end. For once, we had partnered up and were working together.

I had never felt such strength from it before. It didn't hurt, it just felt like it was a part of me now and like my power had momentarily become one with my soul.

I closed my eyes and let the solidarity marinate in every moment we bonded together as I knew the feeling would not last forever and so, as I clenched my fists and the energy poured out of my body, for once in my life, I had no regret about harming something or about letting go of control. My mind and soul were finally free.

The Beginning

You could smell him before he even entered the room.

The potent and familiar concoction that was of beer and pork scratchings lingered around the walls of the house as my father entered our home from another one of his nightly drinking sessions from the pub. A place where he would go to numb the guilt and pain that had tortured him for years.

Only something strange happened that evening as he entered the house. He wasn't his usual abusive self to me. In fact, he didn't even speak. This immediately made me lift my head up off the couch where I had been asleep and aim my eyes in his direction. However, as our gaze met awkwardly for a second, he simply drew his lids closer together and sent a glare to me as he proceeded to pass by the door to head upstairs.

No usual grunts of annoyance nor shouting at me with his drunken slurs.

Nothing, but silence.

The man I hated so dearly headed upstairs and ignored me. Which had never happened when he was drunk. Straight away; I knew something was wrong that night. He wasn't himself, nor should he have been here this early in the evening.

I sat up on the sofa, turning my head to gaze at the clock on the wall that read a mere ten in the evening and tried to figure out what was going on with him. He never arrived home until way after three in the morning.

Had he lost control again? Was he just going upstairs to get his bat to beat me, so he could vent out some of the pain his ability caused him; an ability he could not truly release without causing a danger so big it was too risky to let out? I couldn't tell at all and the wait till I heard his footsteps tread back down the uncarpeted staircase again sent a shiver through my spine. Even more so than usual.

However, to more surprise, nothing happened. Except, just before he left, he stopped at the living room door, not looking at me, and muttered the words that would forever stick in my mind:

"Learn to control the monster inside you."

He soon left our home and headed to his death.

It wasn't until the next morning that I saw his face on the news and I truly found out the reasoning of his calm and strange behaviour. But, it didn't surprise me. He *had* lost control. Finally.

Though it wasn't like the time he burned his mother alive. In fact, his death was not even caused by the same flames that ran through the bloodstream that I had inherited from him, the very supernatural ability he had lived with his entire life and never learned to control.

He had taken his own life after jumping off a bridge. Which was no surprise to me of course, given I had waited for that day to arrive for what felt like a lifetime. Since I'd been born, he'd been haunted by the memory of when he had lost control and burned down his mother's house, killing her. As such, I was surprised he hadn't tried to take his life sooner.

And that's why he beat me—because I reminded him not of my own mother, who took her life when I was five years old, but rather of himself, especially given I had inherited not only his looks but his power. He therefore thought of beating me as destroying himself, so he could try and let out the frustration his past mistakes had made. However, I obviously was no longer a good enough outlet for his pain and he finally decided that death was the only option, the last freeing feeling.

It was a strange day when he died because I wasn't sad nor was I happy. I was nothing. And I think that this was the distinct moment that I became more numbed at the thought of killing and death. It was the moment that triggered my life becoming consumed by our shared power and the road of destruction that would become my entire being, just like he said. That if I did not learn to *control the monster*, it would control me like it did him, and that stage was already arriving.

I did feel that one thing. That this ability, this monster inside me that my father had genetically passed down to me, was going to kill me too, mentally and psychically, just like him, if I didn't learn to control it and soon.

Little did I know, it would be the hardest thing I ever did. And that my father would haunt my life more than I could ever imagine—as I knew that there was a possibility I could turn out just like him. Nothing scared me more.

I just had to hope I had enough fight left in me after it was drained from my soul from the years of abuse. Hell had not ended for me yet, but instead, had just begun.

One

"Here we go again." The words flew out of my mouth effortlessly as I heard my bedroom door crash open. My aunt entering the space with another look of determination to get me out of bed, crinkling her aged face. It was another episode of, *Do What I Think Is Best For My Niece, Even If It Is Not*. I threw my blanket over my head just as the morning sunlight bathed my room with a pool of golden radiance as my Aunt Sylvia stormed her way in and drew back the curtains almost viciously. Something she had begun doing every morning this past week to try and finally get me out of my self-created blanket cocoon. Instead of being happy another morning had dawned upon me, I dreaded entering the real world. As the golden shimmer poured through the cracks of my blanket, I wanted to hide further under my white cotton shield and just dissolve away into my mattress.

"Aunt, get out. I want to sleep," I grumbled from under the covers, even though I had a feeling it was going to be a waste of words today. I had pulled this trick too many times already. The game that was hiding away from my problems.

"Come on," Sylvia groaned back in her familiar stressed tone as I heard her feet shuffle across the wooden flooring and stop beside my bed. I dug further under as she suddenly tried to tug away my blanket and the sunlight spilled in even brighter around the space, projecting her shadow onto the floor with its illumination as my eyes started to peek through the cracks. "You are going to college today whether you like it or not. Now come on, you can't afford to miss another day."

Silence lingered for a few moments before I felt a hand latch around the fabric above my head.

"Lexia, you are seventeen, not seven. I'm not playing this game anymore."

She tugged at the blanket edges even harder to try and snatch it away and after a few more annoying moments of fighting to stay hidden, she sadly succeeded and my barrier flew to the ground. I hissed like a vampire as the brightness that surrounded the room hit my eyes. I sure felt like one of late, seeing as neither my skin nor my eyes had seen the light of day since I had locked myself in my room for so long. Three weeks now and counting. The only times during that period that I did leave was when Sylvia left for work, after giving up on trying to get me out of bed. I would scuttle to the bathroom and then the kitchen to stock up on some food, with my blanket wrapped around me, continuing to be the shield that repelled away my reality. And it had been working—I wasn't thinking of anything. However, given how oddly stern she seemed this morning compared to other attempts this week, I really did have a feeling my time of hiding from reality was up.

"I guess you really shouldn't underestimate the strength of a menopausal woman," I said, calming down my blurred vision and soon zoning in on her standing beside my bed. She looked down at me with a narrowed gaze, hands on hips.

This was probably the most we had looked at each other for the three weeks I had been locked away in my bedroom. And oddly, as I observed her face closely for the first time in all of these avoidances, she looked slightly older. Her skin was swollen and huge bags lay under her usually clear green eyes; I knew they were somewhat my fault, since I had given her plenty of things to stress about and it had taken its toll. Not that I would tell her that, of course. I didn't even have to look in the mirror to know I looked like a rotting corpse, so I had no right to tell my aunt how old she looked.

After I didn't move for a few more moments and pretended to be the corpse I felt I had become, she let out a sigh and began to drag me up and out of bed like a rag doll. During this time, I stopped the use of my limbs to try and stump her, but she didn't care and dragged me downstairs, throwing me into a seat at the kitchen table. I slumped my head down onto the wooden surface just as she was about to thrust a bowl of cereal in front of me.

"Lexia, bloody hell!" she sighed, before pushing me back into the seat and placing the bowl on the table.

"I'm not going," I insisted, sitting back into the seat fully and folding my arms. Feeling like a spoiled child as I glared into the cereal that looked thoroughly unappetising.

"I'm not playing anymore. I've had enough. I told you this was the end of this charade you have been putting up and I meant it. This is the last straw—you either go to college to prove to me you don't need help or you'll have to go to counselling, it's your choice. I'm now at the end of my sanity with all of this."

"I'm not ready for either," I spat back. "I just want to be left alone. Besides, I told you, I haven't been well lately. It's nothing to do with my mental state, it's my ability. It's dangerous for me to go back there. You know it does nothing but fuel my anger, which will amount to no good. It's hard enough trying to keep down this thing inside of me. I don't need the extra stresses of college life."

"You have been in your room for three weeks now, you can't miss any more college. You have been alone enough." She lets out another sigh, a thing that seemed to be her main expression these days. "I know times have been hard lately. However, it's time you moved forward and college will help you do so by focusing your mind elsewhere. Your father did just this—locked himself away when his ability acted up. And what did it do? It made him destroy himself quicker because he never faced his problems. Well, I won't let that happen to you."

I couldn't help but scoff at her words. "Oh yes, let me go back to the place full of nothing but bullying and me almost killing people because of this damned ability I can't control. Which then also reminds me of the man I despise when I do lose it. Oh yes, what a great idea, Sylvia. And don't dare compare me to that man!"

And with that, I slid out my seat and began to head back upstairs with her pleads hanging in the background. However, as I stormed through the hall to head back to my bed haven, she stopped me in my tracks and as she swung me around to face her, I realised I was not getting out of college anymore, given her stern expression.

"This is ending right now. Get upstairs, get ready, grab your bag and be back down here in fifteen minutes, when I will be taking you to college. If you fail to do so, I am driving you instead to the hospital for a mental evaluation. Your father refused it but I won't let you do the same. Your choice." And with that, she turned on her heel and slid back into the kitchen, slamming the door behind her and trying to hide her whimpering frustrations at the fact that another one of her relatives was falling apart. Now I knew I had pushed her too far. I soon ran upstairs and slammed my door shut as well, blasting my music to drown out her cries.

I kick the side of my bed in the hope it would release some of the tension that was building up inside me already, the frustration that was destroying my sanity each day because I couldn't control this thing inside of me. The thing that if I didn't release soon, would destroy everything around me. And that was why I had been avoiding college; because if I put myself in that stressful atmosphere, all the work of suppressing my ability those three weeks would have been useless. It had been a hard time since my father's death. And that had been because I was constantly reminded of the man who had ruined me. I had built up so many frustrations that three weeks ago, I withdrew from everything. Bullies and general annoying youth.

I understood what she was trying to do. Trying to shift my focus onto my studies but college for me was a literal hell-hole. Nothing nice waited for me there but people teasing me because of past things and unfortunately for her, I was in no good shape to be understanding, even though I knew her intentions were good.

However, the images of my father suddenly poured into my mind along with my aunt's words of how he used to lock himself away; it was enough to drag me out of my room to face reality, as there was nothing I hated more than being compared to the man I despised. I did not want to go to college. However, I'd rather deal with that than be compared to him, and I knew she would keep doing that if I didn't go, just because it truly annoyed me. Which, in reality, was pretty low of her, especially as after he passed away, she had discovered that he'd been abusing me for years. It was pretty low indeed. However, it worked and I knew it was her only choice—nothing else was working.

After letting out the world's biggest sigh at the fact I had to leave the house, I stomped towards my bathroom and flung my blonde hair up into a casual bun, washed my face with some cold water and brushed my teeth before heading back into my room, stuffing my bag with my school supplies and getting dressed. It was the first time in ages that I was putting on clothes that weren't my usual monochrome striped pyjamas. I opted for a simple black shift dress and burgundy polo-necked jumper to wear underneath before pulling on my black combat boots, grabbing my phone and heading downstairs, ready to finally get it all over with. On the inside I was crying because I was leaving my bedroom. The only place that I felt safe.

I headed outside and slid into my aunt's car. A few moments later, she came out and sat in the driver's side. Not even acknowledging me as she put on her seat belt and began to drive to college, trying to hide her tears as she did so. I didn't say anything on the journey either, but as we got closer, my stomach suddenly filled with a sickening feeling as I realised I would soon have to face the place I knew would make my power agitated. And I just had an odd feeling something bad was going to happen. That the release day had finally arrived.

You see, release days are my most hated things. In basic terms, when you are born with an ability you can't control, life is not easy. Especially when general society does not even know they exist and have no clue that some supernatural element is eating away at your soul. Since I never use my power nor have great control over my emotions and ability, when these two mix, hell is created in my body and for whatever odd reason, my body feels like it has to let out some of the energy my power creates. This almost calms my soul down. This wouldn't have to happen if I could better control my emotions and power, but sadly, since I cannot, it's something I have had to deal with for many years. Recently, I had got sick of having to let it out all the time and thus, I'd had no release and my emotions were fragile. That is why I locked myself away in my room—I refused to have to release it anymore, as instead of making me feel better and relaxed like it wants to, it reminds me of the past life with my father. I hate this power and the fact I can't control it.

When the car suddenly jolted to an abrupt stop, my train of thought was broken as I saw we were outside the college. I soon found that my little anger burst of enthusiasm was washed away when I saw the swarms of teenagers heading into the grim-looking building.

"I can't believe you are making me do this," I groaned, watching the way too happy teens pass by and trying to control my sudden trembling hands.

"Just get out," she sighed back.

"No, this is crazy. I don't feel good. I have not had a release. You are putting people in danger, you know?" I pleaded, with a sudden change of heart now I was actually here.

"Out!" she yelled and forced me away.

I took a deep breath and jumped out the seat, watching her speed off only seconds later and leaving me to deal with what awaited inside those walls.

I understood why she was frustrated with me. However, she of all people should have known not to test me like this, given her brother was my father. Instead, she had become so hostile with me and I just couldn't understand why my own aunt was disregarding my stress like this. Surely she knew that sending me here wouldn't distract me but do the exact opposite?

I let out a sigh and turned my gaze back to my college and the clock on the front of the building that read 7:55 a.m. The class was about to begin; however, I couldn't take another step forward. It was even worse than I had imagined and as the last groups of teenagers sauntered inside the building, I could feel my breathing become faster and the panic attack rising up in my chest. I just hoped it wasn't the fire that I was actually feeling.

As I stared more intently into the gates, I almost turned away and ran. However, I knew if I didn't attend college again, Sylvia would finally have enough and I truly would be cast aside. She would finally disconnect herself from any relations. Though what really forced me to enter was the thought of my father ditching his education in the past. Again, I couldn't stand the idea of being compared to him.

I clutched my left hand to my right wrist as I felt the pain begin to rumble under my veins, the pain that was telling me to run or something bad was going to happen, but I had to ignore it and hope that I could last till lunchtime. Suppressing it for another day like I had been managing to do. However, I'd only been doing that by hiding away from triggers; I knew this was different.

As I took a deep breath and trekked into class, I hoped for the best that this morning would move fast, so I could take a break and calm my already frayed nerves. I had yet to calm down and that was not a good sign in itself.

***

As the time passed in my first class of the morning, I suddenly started to feel a familiar hot sweat begin to tickle at my skin in the midst of the lesson. Though luckily it was only a passing irritant, and therefore, I decided to forge ahead and go to my next class, which was maths.

However, this was when things began to take the worst turn in my life, ever. And I truly began to regret not clinging tighter to my bed sheet that morning.

I was waiting for this day to happen. The day that everything would change.

There was one word that I now needed to remind myself of and that word is: intuition. A term I wish I had abided by before any of this chaos that was about to erupt into my life had occurred. If I had just listened to my gut feeling that morning, then although this situation may have still arisen at some other time, perhaps it wouldn't have taken place at college, one of the worst possible buildings for me to lose control as there were so many fragile humans roaming the halls.

My aunt had been waiting for this day too. Only for her, it would be the second time she had seen a family member decline and this power, this inherited ability in my body, was now going to take over me and there was nothing I could do. It was the exact same thing that happened to my dad, he let it build up for too long and caused a devastation.

It had happened so many times over the past few weeks yet nothing had occurred. It would rise up in me like a fiery storm poking at my veins to be let out, then settle down for a while again. Therefore, Sylvia wouldn't allow me to miss anymore college as I was already at risk of expulsion. That was why she had been so forceful that morning and so, here I was sitting in maths class, twiddling my fingers nervously through my hair as I waited for the class to end. I needed my lunch break so I could rush to the bathroom and try to calm myself down before something bad happened as the hot sweat from earlier had returned.

I laid my head down on my desk not even caring about the fact other students' gazes dug into me. I suddenly started to feel light-headed, beads of sweat forming on my flushed cheeks as I could feel my ability scratching away at my veins, the fire that I produced gnawing under my flesh to try and escape. It so dearly craved a release so my body could calm down. It was as if it was finally telling me it wasn't going to take no for an answer anymore. And you may think, *"Well if it needs a release, then why not just let it out? Forget about your father"*. How I wished it was that simple.

This was the problem. It was not just about comparing myself to him. Once I let my Pyrokinesis bleed out of my soul, that was it. I wouldn't know when it would stop. When it did pour out of me, nobody would be safe, as I couldn't control the damned thing. The release ban I had placed on myself was not just because I didn't want to be like my father but also because I could destroy so much and had no control of when it stopped.

I never thought this would be me in the future that was for sure. In the past, before my mother committed suicide, we were a pretty normal family. Well, forgetting the supernatural aspect of me and my father, of course. However, other than that, I was a happy enough child. It was just the three of us in a small flat in the centre of our town of Newcastle. My mother had worked in retail and my father at the local bus depot.

We talked, we laughed and we lived, like any other normal family. That was all until my accident and things began to change. The incident that made me see for the first time, I was not normal.

I was at school, isolated in the school playground as usual because people never seemed to like me. Mainly because although my childhood seemed normal, many of the other families didn't think so. My parents were secret alcoholics, you see. I didn't think much of it at that time because I was so young and they were pretty nice to me, generally. However, when I looked back, I would be taken to school in unwashed clothing, my mother would cause arguments with other parents for no reason and generally, my parents weren't great people to be caring for a child. And this opinion soon bled from the parents' minds into those of their children. Soon after they decided my parents were odd, I was labelled it too, and I think that is what caused the build up that day in the playground; why my ability came out at that moment.

I remember the scene so vividly, even though I try not to. I was really sad that day because I had wanted to play with some of the other kids but once again, they just laughed at me and ignored my existence. I sat on the edge of the sandpit by myself, gazing at the scene of playing children and I was jealous I wasn't one of them. I got so lost in the image and could feel my anger rising from how horrid they were treating me; I hardly even paid attention to the group of girls standing in front of me, trying to provoke me like they usually did. It was at that point, I lost it.

My fire blew out of every part of my body for the first time, destroying so much around me that it forced me to pass out. I don't remember much of what happened in the weeks that followed, other than I had seriously injured four of those girls, who now had to live with permanent burns. They had told people about what they had seen, that fire had exploded from me and caused all of this. Of course, nobody would believe such a thing and people were left guessing as to where the fire had come from. Thankfully, people never questioned me.

I had been in a dazed state for weeks afterwards, trying to get my head around what had happened. My mother finally yelled out the words in front of me one day, while having an argument with my father and proclaiming I had inherited his fire ability and that she couldn't live with the fact I had hurt others. Her words froze in her throat as she looked down at me in that moment in our living room, looking shocked I was there and disgusted at me at the same time.

"I got over this in the past, when you killed your mother. However, I can't get over what my own daughter has done. She's not my daughter anymore. I can't live with this."

Those were her last words before she stormed out of our house, never to be seen again. And a few days after that, the abuse began and my father's true personality came to light; he began beating me to a pulp each time our eyes crossed because alcohol was no longer enough to numb him. And all because he was in so much pain.

I shook my head to stop myself from thinking about it, as I knew it would only make me feel worse. Anger and frustration were always the things that triggered it to come faster, like it had in these situations when I was younger. However, I had always managed to hide it in those days, to get away and let the fire pour out without hurting anybody after my first major incident. Those days before my father's death, when I still had an ounce of control. But today, if I didn't get out or calm myself down, then I knew I was in trouble and judging by how I was feeling sicker by the second, I knew it was coming soon.

Eventually, as the clock ticked to just before noon, I grabbed all my supplies and stuffed them into my bag, hoping to just run out of class before the main swarms of teenagers blocked the hallways. However, just as I was about to dart out, my teacher called me to wait till everyone had left. Usually I would have ignored him and just fled. However, by the look on his face that day and how stern his words were, I waited. Which was the biggest mistake I would make.

As I stood by his desk, tapping my foot away as I waited for everyone to leave, I had an odd feeling I knew what was coming: the talk of my bad grades. I had pretty much given up on passing maths class weeks ago, as I had started to have little energy to barely pass the subjects I did enjoy and therefore maths was never going to keep my interest.

As the last student left the room, Mr. McDermid let out a soft sigh and folded his hands over a stack of papers on his desk. His wrinkled skin looking a little more flustered than usual, which I knew was down to the stress I had caused him, judging by what had happened to my aunt's appearance too. I hadn't meant to, it was just that over these weeks everything had begun to decline, and that included my mental state. I could no longer focus on school as it was the least of my problems. Of course, to the teacher, this just meant he would be getting a load of abuse as to why I wasn't handing in projects on time, if at all, or why I wasn't showing up to class as much. And it was all because my ability was destroying me. I had once been a good student—not perfect, but I'd had plans for the future until this blockade was placed in front of me.

He lifted up his tired gaze towards me and I already knew what he was going to say.

"Lexia, you have me very concerned at the moment, like all of your other teachers. Why have you not been showing up to your classes?" He kept his tone low, but I could still sense the frustration behind it. I didn't reply right away, as I'd got lost in my thoughts for a moment; that soon made him slam his hand onto a wad of papers, bringing me back to the scene that was becoming hazy to me.

"Are you listening? I said, if you continue on this spell of avoidances, you won't be here much longer." Mr. McDermid placed his glasses down on the table and looked up with a narrowed gaze. When I didn't reply again, his eyes suddenly widened. "Are you okay, you look like you are about to faint?" he enquired.

I rested my hand against the side of the desk, trying to calm my breathing and not let the haze that was now clouding my vision take over. Luckily, I soon managed to focus myself back into the situation. "Uh, I'm sorry. I've just had a lot going on," I stated simply.

He didn't appreciate my short answer. "Like what? You know you can talk to any of your teachers about your issues, Lexia. Is this about your dad?"

I looked up and met his eyes, feeling anger suddenly pour

through me. Why did they all keep bringing him up, the drunk man I couldn't stand, that had given me nothing but beatings and this damned power I couldn't control?

"Look, it's not about anyone but myself. I get it, okay, I need to come to class more. Can I go now?" I said.

He lets out a sigh. "You know that isn't good enough. I can't have you coming to class in this state. I'm afraid, I think it may be best if you take some time off."

I narrowed my eyes. Even though I had been missing college, I did not want to have to start over and suddenly my back straightened at his words. "Take some time off? No, I finish soon, I can't miss the exams. I'm back now and will work hard." I knew that was a lie since I could hardly focus on things right now, but I was not starting over a term for anything.

"Why is it you suddenly care about them? You are never here to learn what is on them anyway. In fact, I think it's best you start a new term altogether as you have missed so much."

"You can't be serious?!" I almost yelled.

"I'm afraid so," he replied plainly.

"No! I'm not starting over, I want to get away from this place, away from this town that has any connection between me and my dad. I've just had to take some time off because I have been unwell. It's not like it's been a huge amount of time, Mr. McDermid."

"Then, I'm afraid, you'll be expelled if you don't start over."

"This must be a joke."

"I don't understand why you are so surprised, Lexia. You have not learned anything this whole term, how could you possibly take the exams? No, you've finally made my mind up. I think it will be best for you to take a break and gather your mind. I'll be talking to the headmaster tomorrow, to confirm it all. I'm sorry, but it is for the best."

As he said those last words, he began to jot something down on the paper in front of him and as I looked at him with a scowl, I could feel nothing but hatred and knew it was the last straw.

"This is so stupid," I croaked, before swiping off the supplies on his desk out of frustration and slamming my way out the room, knowing that even though I had really brought this upon myself, it wasn't really my fault because something was going on inside me that I couldn't control.

The power that I had no grasp over was destroying me, burning my insides, and there was nothing I could do. There was no way I could start college over again; I hated it here, this town and my aunt somewhat. Everything about this life. I needed to start over and once I had finished college, I had planned to do just that. But now, this ability had begun to take over my life again and was ruining everything. Another reason for me to hate my dad even more.

I stormed out the class and down the slowly filling halls, leaving the teacher's voice calling my name in the background. I soon got to the bathroom and rushed inside the cubicle, thinking I was going to throw up. However, I soon realised what was happening when I went and splashed some cold water on my face and saw my veins glowing with a red tinge. I almost screamed as I glanced at the fiery glow appearing as I knew what was going to happen.

My veins sparkled with a fiery orange light, glowing through my translucent skin and slowly getting brighter as each second passed. It was going to happen, my ability was going to explode out of me and if I didn't get out of this building now, everyone was in danger. I latched up my bag and ran out the bathroom, but sadly as I turned around the corner, I bumped into the last person I needed to see. The person who had played a part in being one of the major stresses of my life.

"Ouch, what the hell!" spat Marissa, the girl who had been intent on giving me abuse pretty much since the first day we had met. That was in primary school, when I humiliated her in year two by doing something as simple as pushing her down in the playground when she got dirt on my favourite shoes. From that day, she had been determined to return the favour of the humiliation she felt when everyone laughed at her, and more. I had apologised countless times, but she was the type of girl to hold huge grudges and thus, had been my bully since that day. This had now taken its toll.

As I felt the heat begin to burn up my throat, I tried to push past her and her snobby group of friends, but she refused to budge.

"Marissa, move out the freaking way!" I yelled, but as I tried to push past again she just kept shoving me back.

"You move, you damn idiot, you owe me a fight!" Marissa squawked, before falling silent when she caught the sight of my golden veins as my shirt sleeve rolled back.

"What the hell is that?" she urged, crinkling up her face with repulsion.

This time I managed to push her slightly out of the way, but by now it was too late. It was coming and made me freeze on the spot. I felt my eyes begin to turn into the orange shade that now flowed through the veins of my pale skin. They sparkled with golden and red hues, which soon couldn't hold themselves inside my fragile body any longer.

As my breathing choked in my throat and I began to haze out, I knew the power was going to explode from me and there was nothing I could do. I knew now that it had all been a mixture of what had led up to this day. So much stress had rained upon my life over these last few weeks that my power was doing what it always had—it was protecting me. I had managed to suppress it from escaping me for so long, but now I couldn't. The bullying, the aggravation, the death of my dad because of this ability and the lack of control. It needed a huge release, it needed to protect me, and no longer was it going to be forced down like I had forced down my emotions. Now was the time not just for a small bout of relief, but a disaster.

My emotions were now too strong for me to control.

My protection mechanism was going to do just that, protect me and I had no choice but to finally let it happen as my mind began to black out from the intensity of the pain.

And before I knew it, the fire erupted from my soul and began to light up the college halls with its fiery beam. I just knew that if I somehow woke up from this tragedy, my life was going to be forever changed.

Two

It was the whimpering sounds of my aunt that first woke me up after the fire had exploded from my fragile body.

Before I even opened my eyes, I could hear her sniffled tears beside me, mumbling to herself that she had lost another family member to this power. I almost wished she had. Because I knew that as soon as I peeled back my eyelids, I would have to face reality and that I would see just how bad what I had caused really was.

I felt strange as I just lay there in silence. I didn't feel pain. In fact, I sort of felt like an odd weight had been lifted off my shoulders. Which I had guessed was the fact that I had finally let my power out. I just wondered exactly how much that was. I knew I had caused a destruction, as even though I had blacked out, I still remembered the halls of my college bursting into flames and the screams beaming around me just before I hazed away.

That memory itself made my eyes force themselves open.

I couldn't believe it had happened. I lurched up in my bed as the images of what destruction I had caused began to pour in. The fire, the screams, the pain, all hitting me like a tidal wave. All confirming that I was turning into my father and the sad reality was, there was nothing I could do, just let it consume me like it did him.

"No!" I yelled, as I looked down at my arms that were still beaming with a slight orange tinge and now raw, truly confirming that I had lost control.

My shout made my aunt suddenly jump up from the seat that was beside my hospital bed and she came to my side, latching her hands onto my shivering ones.

"It happened!" I cried, as the images of the explosion started to pour into my mind.

lm down!" Sylvia pleaded, trying to hold back even ny worried state.

is shouldn't have happened, I tried so hard to not let it continued to bleed down my cheeks, as I felt my ...y begin to panic. It had never been this bad, never so public and never such a huge rush of fire.

"So much fire. I don't understand—why can't I control this damn thing!"

My aunt pushed me back into the bed to try and calm me down, my heart began to slow a little but the tears wouldn't stop.

"Lexia, this isn't your fault. Your father never trained himself nor you on how to use this ability, so this was bound to happen someday. But you need to calm down!"

"I can't! It's happening! I'm turning into him! I'm dying, what am I going to do?!" I shouted through tears.

My aunt put my hands on either side of my face. "You aren't turning into him. I won't let you." She suddenly let out an odd sigh, "That is why I contacted help."

It took me a few seconds to grasp the end of her sentence. "What?" I replied, confused, as she looked at me with a stern gaze.

"You are going to learn to control this ability once and for all. I should have done this years ago," she said, moving to sit back down in the seat beside my hospital bed. For a moment, I just lay there confused, trying to calm myself down before she suddenly continues.

"If only I had heard of this place a long time ago, then none of this would have happened."

"Aunt, I don't understand what you are talking about."

"I've arranged for you to go somewhere. A place that will help you. We will discuss all of it later though, I think it's best that you calm down first and get some sleep."

I let out a sigh. "Sleep, after what I have done? Though, what exactly happened, did anyone get hurt?"

"You don't remember?"

I shook my head. "I only remember a small part before I blacked out: the halls were enveloped with flames and screams surrounded me."

"Well, I'm afraid, something quite bad," she urged, biting her lip nervously.

"What about the people in college? Did I hurt anybody?"

My aunt continued to bite her lip for a moment before continuing, picking her words carefully so I didn't panic again. "Most got out, as they jumped out of the windows. However, a few... didn't make it. But you can't blame yourself, you have this ability inside of you that you can't control. I'm so sorry I forced you to go to college, I never thought it was this bad."

"I killed people, didn't I?" I utter, trying to hold back more tears.

"Your ability did, Lexia."

"What will happen to me, will I be arrested?" I gasped.

Sylvia looked at me peculiarly. "Why on earth would you be arrested? No one knows you have this ability, they just think it was a freak accident."

"But Marissa and her friends did, they were right in front of me when it happened."

"And I'm afraid Marissa and her friends are the ones who died."

I laid my head back on my pillow. It didn't hurt me as much to know it was them I had killed and as harsh as that was, when you've been bullied for almost your whole school life due to one mistake, then I doubt you'd feel very emotional for them either. However, death was not something I wanted on my hands and no matter who it was I killed, I still hated the fact I had hurt people.

"I have arranged for you to get some help. I wish I had known about this place years ago, but it wasn't until recently, when I went through your father's old things, that I found their contact information."

"What are you talking about?" I enquire, turning my face to hers.

"Lucida. A facility that will teach you to control this ability. Anyhow, we will discuss all this when you have had some sleep. As this will all still be so raw right now."

Lucida. The word wasn't familiar. My aunt was right though, I needed some sleep to calm down or I could trigger my power again and since destroying a hospital was not something I wanted to add to my destruction list, I followed her words.

I soon fell back to sleep. This all still felt like a dream and the short burst of panic had knocked me out. Sadly though, I knew that when I woke up, my problems would still be there and I would truly see what my aunt was talking about. I had to face a reality that I never saw coming.

***

It wasn't until three days later, when I finally woke up, that I truly began to recover from the trance I had been placed under. Slowly I began to feel the weight lift off my shoulders and the haze fade. My soul was no longer clogged with energy and as such, I felt a lightness. My veins had nearly returned to their usual blue shade under my skin as well. Though they still held an orange tinge, and red fragments of scorched patches still remained around my hands. How much longer this would last, of my skin healing and getting back to normal, I didn't know. Soon my body would need another release and so, the anticipation once again began of waiting for the glow to fully return.

I knew that this was going to happen to me at some point in my life, just like it had with my father. However, now it had, how could I move forward? My life was just panning out like his and if that continued to be the case, what was the point of carrying on? Knowing that the only future I had was full of pain and sadness thanks to a power I couldn't control was terribly depressing; my messed-up emotions didn't help matters either. At this point, I didn't know what to do other than hope things would turn out okay.

As I lay there, wallowing away in self-pity, they arrived. Lucida.

My aunt forced a smile as she came and sat in the seat next to my bed. "Oh great, you're awake. Lexia, I have some people I would like you to meet."

My eyes drifted towards the front of the room, where two tall men in black suits and a petite woman in the same style stepped inside and quietly closed the door. The woman removed her black tinted shades as she greeted me with a smile and the two men stood behind her, rather sullen. She approached me.

"Who are these people?" I urged through narrowed eyes.

"Remember, when you woke the other morning after the incident and I told you it was time you went to a place to learn how to control your ability? Well, these are the people that will help you do so. They are from Lucida."

"I thought that was a dream," I blinked in surprise.

"No, this is very real, Lexia," said the strange woman, in the most Received Pronunciation accent I had ever heard.

I narrowed my eyes at these people, who stood patiently in front of my hospital bed, still feeling slightly confused as to what was happening. However, as the memory played out of my tired conversation with my frantic aunt when I had first woken here, my eyes soon widened. Lucida, or more so the people who worked at this so-called facility I just recalled her speaking of, soon became a reality.

She came over and stood by the other side of the bed, facing my aunt. The two men just stood near the door like bodyguards or more so, as if what they were trying to tell me was that I didn't dare try to escape. This oddly made me nervous and I clung to the white bedsheet as the woman stared down at me through a cool blue gaze.

I turned my gaze back to my aunt, who had placed her hand over mine, which made me even more worried. "Aunt Sylvia, who are these people?"

My aunt lets out a soft sigh, bypassing my question as she looked over to the woman next to me. "She still seems to be a little dazed, given I'm sure she barely recalls what I said the other night," my aunt said and the woman gave a slight nod.

"Of course, she will be. It was quite an explosion that erupted from her, I imagine she will not be completely back to her senses for a few days yet."

I snatch my hand out of my aunt's grasp. "Stop talking about me as if I'm not in the room. Aunt, who are these people?!"

"Lexia, I just told you. They are from Lucida."

"And who the heck is a Lucida!"

My aunt ignored me again and stood to face the woman. "Maybe it still isn't the right time to tell her. I have already told her about the facility, somewhat. However, she seems to have forgotten."

I slammed my hands down on the blanket, getting annoyed I was being treated so insignificantly. "My memory is fine, I am just tired. Just tell me what Lucida is, you're confusing me."

The woman gave a nod and my aunt looked back down at me. "Lexia, I told you the other evening about the facility that is Lucida. It is a place I want you to go for a few weeks to get back on your feet."

"Facility? Something like a rehab?"

"Not exactly," the smiley woman next to me suddenly interjected. "Lucida is a facility for teens like you, who have lost control or never had control of their ability. Lucida is where they go to do just that, gain control."

I almost wanted to laugh. "Is this a joke?" When nobody's expression broke, I soon gathered it was serious.

"We don't joke about such serious things as this, Lexia. You have caused quite a disturbance in society and we at Lucida are only called out in serious instances."

"You expect me to take this seriously? Are you telling me you work at a place designed to help supernatural youth learn to control their ability? Yeah, because that sounds all so normal."

My aunt slapped me on the side of the arm. "Lexia, stop it with the laughing. This is serious. Miss. Ellewood just told you Lucida only comes out in severe circumstances; realise just how serious this is."

"Then why now, of all times, would you come? I have needed to learn control for years!"

"Because, we only work with cases that have already lost control. As some youth grow up and don't cause any trouble and learn to control their ability on their own, we aren't always needed. We only cater for people that have caused destructions, like yourself."

"Well, how do you know what happened?"

"Your aunt called us."

I turn my eyes with surprise to my aunt. "And why now, of all times, would you call such a place? I have needed to control this thing for years!"

"Did you not just listen to what she said? They only come out when you have caused things like this. I couldn't do anything sooner. Besides, I never even knew this place existed until recently, when I went through your father's things and found their contact information. Contacting them was a last resort."

"If my father knew about such a place, why did he never learn to control his power? He caused plenty of disturbances in society—such as burning down his mother's house, with her in it."

Miss. Ellewood let out a sigh under her breath. "Because he fled. He did stay at our facility when he was younger, after his first destruction, for a short time, but he ran away. Sadly, he never let us help him. However, now you have seen that is not the right thing to do, I urge you to come to Lucida for help, Lexia."

I guess it wasn't surprising my father never stayed at whatever this facility was. He would have had to have faced his demons, which in his case was facing the power that killed his mother, so it wasn't surprising he never stayed there long enough to get better.

"What if I don't go to this place? Will I just turn out like my father, in the end?"

"That is not for us to tell. However, your ability, if left untrained, will only proceed to worsen over time and if you continue to let it rise inside of you, you will cause a much more devastating destruction than what happened at your college. And then you would have a true problem, as you would be locked away without your consent."

"What do you mean?"

My aunt let out a sigh. "What they are saying is that, if you don't go to their facility then in the future, you will be locked away forever as you will be too dangerous to be around humans."

"So, you are telling me this place is my last chance before something really bad happens. Wasn't the college explosion bad enough?"

"Yes, it was actually. And if you had been older, you would have been locked away in a supernatural prison. However, since you are young, we give people like you a chance and so, we suggest you take this break. If you want a future of freedom."

I lay back in my bed for a moment and mulled over her words. They were sounding mighty tempting. Maybe Lucida was just what I needed–a way to escape this town and my aunt for a while. And even though I was going to be locked away with crazy teenagers, maybe it was better to be surrounded by others like me, while at the same time learning to control this monster inside.

"If you don't go, you will wind up dead like your father or locked up," urged Miss. Ellewood.

"What exactly can you do to help?" I enquired.

"We have specialist training facilities that can help. We are a very specialised unit that only deals with the most dangerous and uncontrolled supernatural youth. It's a place that will help you learn to live alongside your ability and conjure it up whenever you choose. Not when it chooses. I don't want to sound threatening, but it is basically your last chance before going to the supernatural prison, Halloway."

Even though I didn't want to be locked away, I knew I needed help. And as the thought of going to this supernatural jail wasn't a prospect I desired, I didn't really have a choice but to agree. Besides, I knew I would lose control again in the future and ultimately it would finally end me.

"Please, Lexia," my aunt urged, "you need to go to this facility, so you don't become like your father and let it consume you. This is your only option or you face becoming him."

I grabbed onto the end of my bedsheet nervously. Finally, the words just slipped out, "I guess I have no choice, do I. If I want to live a normal life."

"You have made the right choice, Lexia," said Miss. Ellewood, as she placed her hand on my shoulder. As she left, I just had to hope that this place, this chance, was finally the start of a happy future and would mean I would never be reminded of my father again.

Three

It had been five days since I had been in the hospital and lots had happened in that short time.

My body had now somewhat recovered and healed from where the fire had ripped out of my veins; my skin was back to being its pale unblemished self. The pain in my chest had moderately soothed too, but it still felt tender. And I had slowly come to terms with the fact I was now a killer. However, at the same time, I still couldn't believe what had occurred.

My aunt had told me more of what had happened in the aftermath of the disaster. That I had been pulled out of the wreck and that people were amazed I had survived and had sustained only minor injuries, especially since the people in the hall with me had burned to a crisp. It caused an odd type of speculation, but it couldn't lead anywhere. At the end of the day, no one was going to believe I had supernaturally created this mess and so thankfully, they took it that a faulty pipe had caught fire. They assumed I had got lucky and somehow survived.

As I had been a recluse and had missed so much college of late, I was soon forgotten about anyway, slipping under the radar as people focused the spotlight on the dead girls instead. They were the well-known faces, after all.

It was all so much to take in. Not just the fact I was now a murderer, but also the images of the burnt-out section of the college, showing the strength of my power and what can happen when I hold it in too long. I knew from there forth, I could never let this happen again.

This had never happened to me before though, on this scale. I had never felt pain like it, emotional or physical. However, I did know it was what could happen if you didn't have control of your ability: you feel it running through you and it messes with you. Though my body had now settled and my mind was not as hyper-emotional anymore, especially after discovering I had hurt people, I glanced down at my arms and saw the veins were still tinged with orange. As healed as they seemed, the sparkle of red lava still shone through slightly, reminding me not to forget what I had done. Seeing my veins like this had utterly confused the doctors, as evidently, no one knew about supernatural abilities. I was just glad that Lucida also had their own abilities and told me not to worry, as all the people's memories would be erased by a member of their team who had seen to me. This was comforting, but weird to think of another person having such an ability. As my father was the only other supernatural I had met, I never really thought about other people's powers.

The people from Lucida soon came back to see me and talked through what would be going to happen once I arrived at the facility. It seemed pretty daunting. Endless bouts of training sessions to make up for years of power neglect and once I entered the place, I wasn't leaving until I had control. But, in reality, I had no choice but to face it. Also, I had to remind myself, if I could get through the hell of a life I'd had so far—the abuse from my father, the death of my mother, the endless nights of wondering what hell lay in store for me next—then I could get through anything.

The next day I got ready to leave and said goodbye to my teary aunt at the hospital. She had packed a bag for me as I was heading straight to my new life at Lucida. And I was actually glad to have this break from her, as although I thanked her for raising me since my father's suicide, her protectiveness over me and trying to get my life on a new path after learning he had abused me had been so overbearing that I was glad to have a break.

On the way to the facility, my nervousness was slowly replaced by a curiosity as to what the place would be like. I actually had a burning question in my mind, about myself, as we headed there, and decided to ask one of the two men who were driving me. I knew one of them had an ability as he had been the one to erase the memories of the people at the hospital.

"Can I ask you a question?" I said, staring out into the front seat.

The man nodded, as he glanced at me through the rear-view mirror. "Of course."

"Why can't I control this ability? I mean, I know I've had no training in the past to be able to. However, shouldn't I be able to at least have some control and not let it just explode from me at random moments? I used to be able to just about manage to do that, though for some reason as I've gotten older, I can't anymore."

"Well, I was lucky to be born with control. However, not everybody is. Because every ability is different. Some are stronger than others. It's also about how you are programmed inside and I guess we can say your genetic coding, just like your father's, is messed up when it came to the control parts. That's why, as you have gotten older, it has been harder to suppress it; stress becomes more apparent as we age and I can see that in your case, like many other supernatural youths who can't control their ability, anger, confusion, and stress have triggered your ability and made it too much for you to handle. It reacted by doing what it was brought to you for— it protected you. So, it sees itself as doing that, but it doesn't always do it when you want. It's leaking out of you not when you command it to but, well, whenever it sees any amount of stress. It views that as time to explode.

"But, surely not all supernaturals get training when they are young and I'm sure many kids' parents don't even know their child has an ability. So, how do most kids somehow manage it and others, like me, don't? How did you?"

"Like I said, it's all about your genetic coding and sadly in that place, I was lucky to gain full control of being able to erase memories as I got older. You have sadly been one of the few whose control signals have faltered. It's the luck of the draw really. Besides, most kids don't have an ability as strong as yours. Pyrokinesis is a very rare thing and therefore, if not cared for, can be a very dangerous weapon. That is why you made the right decision coming here."

I gave a slight nod before turning my gaze back out onto the passing scenery through the tinted black glass. *The luck of the draw.* That certainly seemed true. I guess, the more powerful the ability, the harder it is to control or, in reality, it was all about genetics.

As the journey to Lucida was so long, thoughts couldn't help but race through my mind as we passed through green countryside. It was safe to say that the journey to Lucida was strange, as the closer I got, my curiosity soon turned back into nerves. Not only was I leaving a whole life behind, but I would be meeting others who understood me, who had gifts like me that they couldn't control, and it would be odd to see these abilities. I had actually started to get nervously excited at the prospect. However, I had to remind myself what the man had told me—that these students were like me. Misfits who had caused bad situations too. I had to be cautious because I had yet to see what these kids were actually like and what 'disturbances' he meant. Mine was an accident but that did not mean that theirs were.

This is what I needed though: a fresh start, away from people who knew me and a place where I could learn to control this power inside of me. A place that could stop me using alcohol to try to hide the fact I wasn't normal, like my dad had done.

Even though I hated how my aunt used to compare us, I knew she was right, I was turning into him. Our ability was too strong for either of our undeveloped supernatural minds and if you didn't learn to control it, then it controlled you. Once that happens, it's only a matter of time before it destroys you, as the power needs a release in some form and if you store it inside yourself all the time, you are a ticking time bomb.

I watched the scenery pass by. It finally dawned on me that this was happening when I stared up at the old-styled building that lay in the desolate lands of an abandoned field in the English countryside. Written on a sign next to it in bold black letters were the words: *Lucida Facility*. This was the place I would have to spend the next few months of my life. A sense of dread couldn't help but waver through me at the thought and my grip on my small suitcase tightened as I slid out of the car. Even though I was somewhat excited at the prospect of a future I never thought I'd have, I still couldn't help but be nervous.

The state of the place on the outside didn't make me feel any better either. As we drove up here I thought we had taken a wrong turning as not only was the facility in the middle of nowhere, but it looked from the outside like it had fallen apart. I mean, they had told me it was supposed to be hidden away, but this was ridiculous.

The building had all the windows closed off with wooden boards. Where the wood had chipped off and rotted away, pigeons had taken it as the best place to nest inside the gaps. The bricks that somehow held the structure together just looked like they would give way at any moment and generally, the surroundings of the huge building were dead. Nothing but acres and acres of dead grass and trees that looked like they hadn't seen water in years. And to top off the creepy aesthetic, we were surrounded by a never-ending high-railed fence so you knew that once you were inside, there was no escape.

I didn't want to be here and I could escape if I wanted, but I had made an agreement and I had to stick with it.

As Miss. Ellewood suddenly called for me to enter the facility, I parted ways with the guards and headed into my new home, nervously gripping my suitcase as I took one last glimpse at the nothingness that surrounded the facility. However, as I entered into the actual building, I couldn't believe the transformation.

I never expected this place to look quite so high-tech and modern, given its external dreary appearance. As the huge cast iron doors closed behind us, we entered into a reception area, where Miss. Ellewood now seemed to match the pristine exterior. Her all-white suit was the same shade as everything else, from the waiting seats to the reception; even the computer was the same tone. Everything had an oddly polished glisten to it, which sent a shiver down my spine. We walked over to a reception area where a woman sat behind the pristine desk; she talked for a moment with Miss. Ellewood before opening the main door for us to enter. The fact that it was not a manual door made me start to feel uneasy again, as I realised just how technical and hidden this place was.

We continued to walk in silence up a flight of stairs that led to a different section of the building, trudging through more gleaming white halls. We stopped outside another main door, on which a sign read *Training and Dorm*, which immediately made this place feel so much more real.

After we went through another automated checkpoint we eventually stopped at a door that read *Dr Henry Lincoln*. I recognised the name from the pamphlet I was given before coming here, alongside the list of doctors. The leaflet itself told me nothing more than who had founded Lucida—which had been an old man named Ezra Lucida, who had died in 1968—and what they did to help supernaturals who had lost control. I remembered from the list that Henry was one of the main doctors at Lucida; he set out what training each individual would do and was most qualified to deal with supernaturals.

Miss. Ellewood knocked on the door twice before a muffled "Yes" came from the other side and as we entered, an older man greeted us with a rather flustered appearance.

"Hi, Dr. Lincoln, our new student has arrived," said Miss. Ellewood, who led me inside as the greying man headed back to his desk, soon turning back on his heel to face me when she had finished. Though I couldn't help but think that 'student' was a nicer way of saying juvenile criminal as I entered.

"Our new student, eh? Welcome to Lucida," Dr. Lincoln suddenly beamed as he came to shake my hand. "It's nice to finally meet you. Please take a seat."

I shook his hand back before taking a seat in front of his cluttered antique desk, which was filled to the brim with paperwork and psychology books. This room was styled quite differently to the rest of the building and looked like we had suddenly walked back in time. The walls were painted a dark maroon shade, and books and objects lay sprawled around whatever space they could. It reminded me of a place a mad scientist would reside while trying to create a monster, which wasn't a comforting thought given where we were and his style of clothing, which included a long white lab coat. His greying, unkempt hair and his pale aged complexion also didn't help

Dr. Lincoln seemed to sense my eyes gazing around at the mess and laughed. "Sorry about all the clutter, I've been too busy to clean it up," he smiled, gazing at the scattered pile of books. "Anyway, let's get on, shall we? I'm sure you want to get settled into your dorm."

I smiled politely back; more than anything, I just wanted to get the whole thing over with so that I could take a nap, as the journey had exhausted me.

He took a seat behind the desk, clearing his throat before speaking. "Now, you do completely understand the reason for you being here, don't you Lexia? Because it's important, in order for you to grow while you are here, to be fully aware of what triggered your powers in the first place and made you completely lose control."

I nodded in response and put on a fake smile. "I do understand. And I'm determined to work hard while I am here, to gain control."

Dr. Lincoln smiled, pushing his glasses closer to his speckled brown eyes. "I'm glad to hear it. Now, here is your training list, which will begin once you have had your evaluation tomorrow. That is just something we do before we begin training so we can place you on the right level. Levels start at one and go all the way to twelve: one being the lowest amount of control and twelve being the most. Once we have seen your ability, we will choose the right level for you and slowly begin to build up your control." He shuffled through some paper on his cluttered desk, before handing me a schedule. On it was all the training that I would have to complete before I could leave. As my eyes scanned the sheet, I gulped at the volume of things I would have to do just to be released. It did not state the level I was at yet of course, as I had yet to be evaluated.

The schedule stated we would have to work from Monday to Friday, getting up at seven in the morning each day to have breakfast before our training sessions started at eight. These would go on until twelve, when we would have lunch and two hours of self-study about our abilities, followed by some more training until five. I wished I could just tear up the paper right there and then, chuck it in his face and leave into the wilderness, but sadly, I had to face reality.

"I know it may seem like a lot, but you will get through it in no time. Now, I'm sure you would like to go and settle into your room and meet your other classmates. We'll be sure to get properly acquainted some more this week, once you have had some rest and settled in. Are there any questions you would like to ask before you head to your dorm?"

I sat on the edge of the seat, pretty much having a million questions running through my mind. Or should I say, a million ways to ask how to get out of here fast, though I didn't bother enquiring, as I knew it wouldn't be the sort of questions he meant. Instead, I just let out a soft sigh under my breath before faking a smile again, trying to look positive even though I felt like death and was slightly unnerved at how fast this was all going.

"No, I think all my questions were answered during the few days I met with the Lucida team who arranged for me to be here. I know what to expect and everything. I just want to thank you all for giving me this chance to change my life and not judging me as a murderer."

"Well, that's good then. And we never judge here, Lexia—we are a place to help youth like yourself. It's great to have you on board Miss. Luccen and I'm sure you'll have a great time here meeting other teenagers who have gone through similar situations as you. Your new life will begin in no time."

We all stood and he offered his hand again to shake, then we head back to the door and he waved us off as Miss. Ellewood led us out. I was glad in a way that the introduction was short, but I couldn't tell whether I liked him or not. He didn't seem a bad guy at first impressions, but in my books, anybody who works for a government facility lacks a part of something in their brain. I mean, who would want to sign away their life and live in a place like this, holding nothing but secrets from their family?

I let out a sigh before putting him to the back of my mind for now, as we headed through another bolted door before eventually reaching the dormitory. It was guarded by a huge double steel grey entryway and as the woman swiped a card to enter, I almost fell back in shock at how the inside was decorated—something that had seemed to become a theme since I had walked inside the building.

We walked into the white gleaming space—to no surprise of course, the same shade as everywhere else throughout—and the whole place shone from marble floor tiles to the silver chandelier that hung from the ceiling. Huge glass windows spanned the whole length of one side of the room, even though you couldn't see out of them as they were blocked by some blurred covering.

Further inside was even grander and green velvet sofas were positioned around a fire pit in the middle of the room, the most ultra-modern style I had ever seen. In the various corners lay vending machines, a ping pong table and games consoles. Finally, a small staircase headed up a wall that was lined with antique bookshelves and stacked to the brim with hundreds of novels I was intrigued to take a look at.

I wanted to gasp, as I had never expected this kind of thing. I had imagined a crummy old falling apart farmhouse that would need some major DIY, but never this.

"This is the dormitory?" I gaped, still in awe of the place as we walked further inside, running my hand along the expensive-looking velvet sofa.

"Grand, isn't it? Dr. Lincoln wanted you all to live in an amazing space and so designed this for you all," said Miss. Ellewood.

"It's grand alright," I said through raised brows. Though I did find this all way to lavish for a group of teens who had supposedly done bad things in society. Not that I was going to complain, of course.

"I'm sure you can take a good look around later, when the other students arrive back from their training. Let's head to your room, shall we?"

I followed her through the room, still trying to pick my mouth up from the floor.

She led me to a door that lay under the bookshelves; it took us to a smaller square space, where three doors lay on each side and two more in front. She stopped at the third door down to the left, fumbled to find a key, and then unlocked it to find an even cooler space.

"Wow, this is amazing! My room at home couldn't even match up to this." It was so true, my aunt and I lived in a small terraced house in the centre of town and as the rent was so expensive, we couldn't afford any luxuries. However, here they had provided a computer for studying, a TV and even a wardrobe full of clothes. It was still gleaming white in here, but a double bed took up most of the space and a desk was planted right in front of another blocked-out window.

"It truly is a great place and I know you will love it here. We wanted you all to feel at home and so decorated the way we thought you all deserved."

After a moment of admiring the room, Miss. Ellewood headed to the door. "Now, you should just get settled in tonight, as we begin training bright and early tomorrow, so make sure to get some sleep. I know you will love it here and I'm sure you'll be in control again soon. If you need me, by the way, I'm your supervisor here. You can give me a call on the phone in the living area at any time, okay?"

After I gave her a nod in response, she disappeared out of sight and finally I could relax.

I took a deep breath, finally realising that this was all happening. I was here and would be for a long time. It was strange—I thought I would have felt a lot worse and my anger would have played up again. However, now I had seen the place, I was beginning to think I could get used to this.

After a few more moments of appreciating my new room, wondering how on earth this place was to rehabilitate delinquents, I decided to take a look back in the common room to make sure what I had seen a moment ago was actually real. Just when I was about to turn the corner and head back into the main space, I suddenly heard an almighty scream coming from the room.

It was a girl's voice and as I went to see what was going on, I walked into a sight I never expected to see. A tall guy with black, crazily-spiked hair was standing over a girl who was laying in the main doorway. As he leaned over her, a bright blue bolt of electricity was shooting through his hand.

"Help!" the girl screamed, as she tried to wriggle out of his grasp.

"I told you to freaking leave me alone! It's your own fault!" the boy yelled, the electricity blaring even brighter in his hand. I stood there in shock, not knowing how to respond.

A sudden voice shouted from the hall. "Xavier! Stop! Or you'll end up back at square one!"

Xavier quickly turned his head to the calling voice. "I don't care, this idiot deserves to be fried!" The girl then suddenly screamed even more as the electric blue bolt continued to get even brighter.

I narrowed my eyes at the performance in front of me. However, when he looked up at me suddenly and our gazes met, I felt a strange feeling wave through me and my back straightened immediately.

"Who are you?" he urged as his eyes scanned my frame. As he kept his concentration on me, he was suddenly shot in the neck with a needle. Instantly the blue flame in his hand started to trickle away and his body fell to the ground with a thump.

The girl immediately got up and rushed down the hall, screaming all the way. I froze on the spot, not truly understanding what I had just witnessed.

"Welcome to the crazy house," the guard shouted as he saw me gawking at him in shock, before he dragged Xavier's limp body away, leaving me there to wallow away in the moment. This place truly was going to be an experience.

Four

Not waking up halfway through the middle of the night to hear my father's drunken yells in the form of a nightmare anymore, for the first time in four years, was absolute bliss and made me even more determined to try and create a better life for myself. Without being around anybody who would constantly compare me to my father.

I shook my head and told myself to wipe him and everything to do with him out of my memory from here forth, as it was nothing to me now.

Alongside the undisturbed sleep, I woke up still not truly knowing whether what I had witnessed last night was a dream or something that actually happened. I had never seen another supernatural being use their powers before and it was such a shock to see them being used so openly, right in front of my eyes.

I had lived in such a world of solitude when it came to my abilities that seeing someone using it so blatantly in front of me, for whatever reason it may have been, was a strange thing to comprehend. Also, I finally realised I wasn't alone. And even though I had known I would be with these types of people, I didn't realise how crazy it truly would be to see a blue bolt of light crackling out of someone's palm. Which was strange, given I produce fire, but nonetheless it was still amazing to see another person's ability. It verified the fact that I was not the only mutant alive in this world.

Letting out a sigh at the prospect that day one had finally arrived, I slid out of bed and grabbed some clothes from my wardrobe. I didn't know if there was a dress code, so I opted for a casual style of black jeans and burgundy long-sleeved t-shirt, making sure the sleeves were long enough to hide the burned veins on my arms. Also, it was insanely cold in here; the only weakness of the interior design I had noticed so far.

Grabbing my toiletry bag and towel, I began to head to the bathroom to get dressed, though I soon realised I had no clue where it was. The dorm space was literally just a courtyard full of grey painted rooms so I walked back into the main common area to see if I could locate it. As I did so, I walked straight into someone's chest. Dropping all my stuff as my rather pointy nose—the one my mother sadly had endowed upon me—felt like it had been crushed from the impact.

"Ow, bloody hell," I yelped, clutching my nose which now felt broken.

"Woah, didn't see you coming," called back a deep voice. As I looked up in annoyance, a tall guy stared down at me. He looked rather pleased to see me even though I had never met him before.

"It's fine," I groaned, as I went to pick up my belongings, our heads now clashing against each other as he bent down at the same time.

"You trying to knock me out or something?" I groaned, as we both clutched our bruised foreheads.

"Well, that wasn't my intention. However, it seems to be this morning."

I couldn't help but let out a half laugh as I picked up some of my things and he handed the rest over to me.

"You are the new girl, aren't you?"

"What made you think that?" I joked.

"Well, considering I've been here for a long time now, I'm sure I would have remembered you. Especially, someone with a face as pretty as yours."

I raise a brow and at the same time, cringe a little at his choice of words. "Yes, that would be strange if you hadn't. And thank you, but I don't know if I can return that compliment." We both smirked back in chorus, especially since he was actually good-looking and I was trying my best not to blush at his chiseled bare torso that was only inches away from my face.

"So, why were you in such a hurry?" he asked, bringing me back to reality as he ran his hand through his brunette hair that fell lightly against his forehead.

"I can't find the bathroom," I laughed.

"Yeah, I had that problem at first too. There are no signs or anything." He suddenly grabbed me by the wrist and dragged me into the main common room. "It's right there. Girls to the left," he said and beamed another pearly white smile.

"Well, thanks," I said, heading inside. "Oh, and make sure you bloody look where you are going next time, yeah?" The corner of my mouth curled into a smile and he gave a nod back.

"Will do. And if you need any more help, you can find me in room two to the right. I'll be glad to give you some assistance." He gave a cheeky wink as he headed through to the dorm room.

My smile soon faded away as I looked at my ghastly appearance in the bathroom mirror. I had hardly slept for the past few days due to the stress of coming here and it sure showed. Dark circles lay heavy under my blue eyes, my pale skin seemingly making them look even more prominent. I rolled my eyes at my face, placing my hands against my cheeks and squeezing them together in annoyance before I sighed and headed to take a quick shower. Throwing on my clothes as I got out, I simply combed through my blonde locks with my fingers, brushing past the makeup as I was still in no mood to care about my terrible complexion. I had too many bigger problems to deal with.

After putting away my laundry, I headed back out into the main room, where a group of voices emerged from the kitchen. As I went to investigate, most eyes shifted onto me. Aside from the familiar gaze of the guy I had just met, who was now smiling at me, there was also the girl who had been screaming on the floor yesterday, who now looked nothing like someone who had been electrocuted less than twenty-four hours ago.

Just as I stared at her in confusion, a voice suddenly yelled from the group, sending a shock through me.

"The new girl is here!" yelled an eager guy, who was sitting at the table. His floppy blonde hair flayed about as he suddenly jumped up and threw me into a hug.

"Get off me!" I urged and pushed him back, but he remained unfazed as his brown eyes gleamed at me with excitement.

"Hey, we've been waiting for you for a while, as we heard you have a pretty cool gift."

I narrowed my eyes at him. "Who exactly told you that?"

"It doesn't matter, but I'm glad you are here, it's nice to see a new face. Can't wait to see your ability." He dragged me to sit at the table, throwing a bowl of cereal in front of me moments later as he continued to talk at a thousand miles an hour. "I would eat up if I was you, the training is pretty intensive so you need your strength." For a moment, I was almost going to punch the dude for how annoying he was, but thankfully, the guy I bumped into earlier pushed him out the room.

"Colt, leave the damn girl alone and go get ready, alright."

"But... I just want to get to know her..." he muttered, his face crumbling.

"And you will, later, now just bloody leave before I make you."

And with that, Colt sulked out of the room.

"Sorry about that. He's kind of addicted to girls."

"He's a pervert you mean," chirped a soft voice. My eyes turned in its direction and found it belonged to the oddly relaxed girl, who didn't even lift her eyes up from her magazine as she spoke. As she entered my mind again, so did the blue bolt guy. I gazed around but I couldn't see him at all, which made me curious as to where he was.

The guy I bumped into earlier suddenly came and sat next to me, putting out his hand. "Ignore Elisa, she's just miserable by nature. Or more so, she doesn't care for newcomers," he smiled. "Anyhow, I forgot to tell you my name earlier. It's Hunter Aldrige."

I shook it back. "Nice to meet you, Hunter. I'm Lexia Luccen," I said through a smile. I did feel a strange vibe coming from Hunter as our hands met; he had a pleasant enough aura, but given this was a place for troubled supernatural teens, I didn't know whether to believe this nice act was real or put on and oddly appreciated Elisa for being upfront about not caring for me simply because I was new. However, given I had practically just arrived, I held back my judgements for now.

"Ignore Colt too by the way, he's just a little eccentric, but pretty harmless."

"*Really?*" I said sarcastically.

"Yeah," he nodded through a half laugh. "Anyway, you really better eat up, as I remember I didn't on the first day of training and I passed out from how much we had to do. Though your training probably won't begin until tomorrow because they do evaluations first. I forgot about that. Anyhow, welcome and I'm sure we'll all get properly introduced later."

Hunter put a hand to my shoulder before leaving the room, the miserable Elisa soon following behind him, not even giving a glance my way. I brushed it off and dug into the cereal, just hoping the first day, or tomorrow, wasn't as grueling as he had said.

***

After the crazy start to the morning, I couldn't believe I was being thrown into this world of learning to control my ability so quickly. However, given I was in a dangerous way right now, I needed to get the evaluation over with before I could even begin a training plan. I understood the evaluation was needed as they wanted to make sure whatever training I was given was attuned to myself rather than a pre-made programme. Therefore, I supposed the sooner I trained, the better. It was best to get this evaluation over with so they could begin to do just that. I just really hoped they did not make me conjure up my ability so soon as then, we would have a problem.

With my new group of roommates accompanying me, we headed off to the training facility, which was only a short walk down the hall from our dorm. And as soon as Miss. Ellewood swiped her card for us to enter, I was stunned once again, this time by the amount of technology that was spread out in front of me.

The main area was a huge rectangular space, inside which must have been hundreds of high-tech machines. I had no clue what they were used for, but they were scattered messily all over the marble tiled flooring. There were also ten doors spaced around three of the facing walls of the rectangular room; the other students had been directed through these, the doors closing behind them so I couldn't see their abilities. However, on some of the rooms there were windows attached so you could see inside and so, as I passed them by, I caught glimpses of them beginning to conjure up whatever abilities they had.

It was a short blip of observation though as after walking through a portion of the gleaming white technical space, I was assigned two members of staff by Miss. Ellewood, who had greeted me upon arrival to the training space. The two staff members being a man and woman named David and Emma, who had to have been in their late thirties. Both greeted me coldly and the man seemed in a rush to lead me into a smaller room, at the farthest part of the space, where there was nothing but me and the four walls and of course, the window facing. After telling me to sit at a small wooden table, David pulled an odd little machine from his pocket, pulled out wires from it, and attached white electrodes to my forehead and wrists with stickers, before placing the machine on the floor beside me and heading back out the room, to stand in front of the large window that was facing me.

"Now, Lexia," shouted Emma through an intercom, pushing her glasses closer to her eyes as she looked at me intently. "What we want you to do is a simple test, to show us the strength of your ability so we can see what we are working with. We need to be able to put you on the right training level before we begin the official training. All you have to do is let your ability flow out of you and just do the best you can."

I shake my head in annoyance, as although I knew I would be unleashing my power here, never did I think it would be this soon after the catastrophe. Also, by the way she was talking about it, she wanted to see more from me than I could give. "I can't do this yet. I can't control my ability, it's dangerous for me to open it up doing something as intensive as this; just letting it out naturally."

"It's fine. The booth is strong, just do what you can but still, we need to see some impact. We just need to evaluate your power, to be able to put you on the right course of treatment."

"I'm serious, it's dangerous, it's still so soon. Look at my veins," I urged again, showing my slightly burnt arms, but I could feel my words were being wasted since they seemed to be in such a hurry to get this over with. They both exchanged glances, ignoring my statement. I really couldn't control my ability and given the reason I was here, they knew that. This was too much too fast but I knew they wouldn't budge and so, I had no choice but to conjure up my power.

I took a deep breath and focused to the centre point in the room, trying to keep my breathing calm and level as I felt the energy start to warm up. It was like imagining a ball of fire heating up in your body and slowly adding more and more to it, to make it grow. And for the most part, I could control it. Till the strength got to about half way—after that point, there had never been a good outcome, as I lost control.

My breathing started to pick up and my heartbeat faster. Beads of sweat slowly began to form on my forehead as everything around me started to set alight. And from there, it all went wrong.

The fire began to erupt around me in small bursts and my eyes started to go hazy; everything started to blur out and the power started to take me over. My breathing became rapid, I could hardly catch my breath anymore as the strength began to build and build. It was happening again, the same feeling I had when I destroyed my college.

"Lexia, that is enough now, you may stop," Emma yelled over the intercom. However, it was too late and my power was the one now controlling me. My hands tingled with the prickling sensation and I knew if they didn't stop, this place and everyone inside would be dead. I didn't always have to pass out before it erupted.

Everything around me began to spark brighter with each second and Emma kept yelling stop, but I couldn't anymore. I could feel the whole room was going to explode at any moment. However, just before that was about to happen, I heard the door creak open at the side of me and felt a sudden sharp pain stab into the skin on my neck.

Everything suddenly comes to a crashing halt. My body slowly gave way and my mind slipped into a hazy darkness that had consumed me unwillingly, once again.

Five

"I thought I had it bad, but man, she has won that title for sure," a familiar voice said as my mind started to wake from the coma I had been placed under. As my eyelids slowly peeled back, the white lights that lay above streaming in, I woke to see a group of people gazing down at me curiously.

"She is awake," Colt suddenly beamed by my side, his dimpled smile seemingly creasing with relief as I gazed around the room in my dazed state.

I glanced around to see two of my other roommates and the two staff members staring down at me and I quickly sat up in shock to see what was going on. Then the memory fragments piece back together in my mind as it cleared, of my almost destruction. I turned my gaze back angrily to one of the staff members who had caused the near disaster; he stood behind the group, looking nervous.

"I told you it would be dangerous!" I yelled, as I took a glance at the destroyed room that I could see peeking through the doorway. The walls were stained with grey slash marks and the floor had a huge crack in the centre that bled out the room slightly, like tree roots.

They both flinched back and looked down at me nervously. "We were just going by what is written down, this isn't our fault. Everything is fine, so don't worry," Emma stated. Before I could respond, she looked over to Elisa and continued, "Elisa, please bring her a cup of tea and help calm her down. She will be fine soon enough." And with that, Emma and David sauntered out of the training room, leaving me to process what had just happened.

"I don't feel too good," I said. A sickening feeling suddenly churned in my stomach, an aching pain burning at my neck. Elisa soon brought over a mug of tea and she and Colt both surrounded me.

"That will be the medicine," said Colt, taking the mug from Elisa and placing it by my side, as he came and sat down next to me and placed an arm around my shoulder. "I know how you are feeling. I had the same reaction from that medicine when I lost control one time. Thought when I made that girl guard go insane I was the worst guy in the world and deserved to die after I woke up, but it only lasted a couple of hours and I soon didn't care anymore. Apparently, it raises your hormones for a while so you have odd reactions. Don't worry, you soon won't care."

Elisa narrowed her eyes to Colt. "Yeah, but you should care after what you've done, you sick pervert."

"Hey, don't attack me Elisa, it was an accident. I didn't mean to make her go crazy for me, you can't help who you fall in love with. Besides, she led me on," he added, putting his hand sarcastically to his heart.

"Except she didn't fall in love with you, you bloody drugged her with the curse you attempted to put on her!" Elisa shouted back.

Annoyed with the bickering, I shrugged off Colt's arm and let out a sigh. "Look, shut up, both of you. Back on topic, I don't care about what just happened nor if I hurt them. I'm just angry with those two idiots for making me use my power at that level when they know I can't. Knowing full well the reason that brought me here—to help me gain control so I will be able to use it to that extent in the future, but slowly. Not bloody right now after I just got here."

"Great, so we have another emotionless idiot living here," mumbled Elisa, rolling her brown eyes in my direction, which, nearly made me throw the cup of tea at her out of annoyance.

I soon sent a glare her way instead. "I'm not emotionless. I just can't stand stupid fools like them, who don't listen nor do their job properly. Why should I care if they live or die when they test me like that?"

She scoffed, "It's called being human."

"Elisa, leave her be. Her emotions will be going rampant right now. You know how horrid that medicine is till it wears off," urged Colt.

Elisa just rolled her eyes again and folded her arms like the moody teenager she was. I could tell already she was going to be a pain to deal with.

As my mind had cleared a little more, I soon picked up on the word *medicine* more vividly this time. "Medicine? Are you talking about that needle I felt before I passed out?"

They both nodded back in chorus.

"I see, so that explains why I feel like someone has stabbed me in the neck. Good timing, they got me to sleep fast enough or you may all be dead right now."

Suddenly, our conversation was interrupted by the patter of lone heels walking into the room and as I looked up from the ground, I saw Miss. Ellewood walking in graciously, carrying a wad of papers under her arm. She just stood there for a moment and cleared her throat, trying not to look so nervous as she looked from the mess to me. "Well, what has happened here?" she enquired, trying to hide her panicked tone.

"Your two idiot staff made me almost blow this place up, is what," I spat, while trying to rub away the aching pain I felt in my neck.

"Well, I'm sure it was an accident." She pushed her glasses closer to her brown eyes and gazed down at a piece of paper amongst the wad that had been under her arm. "Ah yes, it says you are on a higher evaluation level then you should be. It was a misprint."

It annoyed me how casually she disregarded it. "And why didn't you check that before we began?!"

"These things happen, I'm afraid."

"I could have blown the place up!"

"I understand, Lexia. However, we'll take you back down to an easier evaluation and you'll be fine. Just like training, we have different evaluation levels to see your ability and it's been put down wrong."

"Fine. Just don't let it happen again or this place really will burn down because you'll have annoyed me," I groaned, though I knew had to be careful, as I didn't want to head to *Halloway Prison,* like they had threatened at the hospital. In reality, this was only a chance they had given me and prison was still where I could have been headed. Even if this time it wasn't my fault, I knew I still had to be more careful from now on.

"I'm sure that won't be the case, Lexia. Anyhow," she said, grabbing Elisa's blouse, "Lexia, I think it's best you go and get some rest and we will resume on the correct level tomorrow. Elisa, will you be so kind as to guide Lexia back to the dorm to rest and make sure she gets plenty to drink, to wash the medicine out of her system."

Elisa sighed before giving a nod and walking straight to the door. I followed behind her as we headed back, clutching my now aching head as we did so. I couldn't believe they made me use my powers like that, after knowing I practically blew up my college—and only a few days ago at that! Even if it was a mistake, it wasn't like there were many students here to begin with, so this shouldn't have happened. I wasn't going to let this go that was for sure. I was going to see Dr. Lincoln, to ask why such a mistake had been made. This wasn't even the training stage yet, after all.

As we headed back to the dorm, Elisa kept silent and to try and forget what just happened, I decided to investigate the strange happening I had witnessed yesterday, between her and the electricity boy.

"So, Elisa... How long have you been here?" I enquired, trying to slowly edge in the question.

She didn't look at me as she replied. "About a month."

"I see. So, do you enjoy it here?"

This time she laughed. "Hell no! We have to get up at these damn crazy times and basically train till we are about to pass out. But I suppose it could be worse."

"I see, so what happened yesterday?" I said, too curious to hold back the question any longer.

"You saw that then, hmm?"

I nodded. "Yeah, it was quite a shock. I've never really seen another supernatural use their powers in real life before."

"Really? Well, you'll soon see too much of it and to answer your question, that guy is just an idiot. He was just threatening me because I ran off with his necklace as a joke, tried to electrocute me just because of that. What a freak. My advice: stay away from him."

"Whoa, how dramatic," I replied. At least I knew never to pull a trick like that on the guy.
"I didn't see him today, did they take him away or something?"

She shrugged her shoulders. "He is hardly here anyway because he gets into so many fights with everyone, all over little things. I heard they just lock him away in a room for a few days till he calms down, then he comes back. Which is crazy since he has nearly killed us all, but what can you do."

My eyes widened a little by the way she replies, it all seems so normal to her, which doesn't exactly sit well with me. However, just like she said, what could I do? As we arrived back at the common room, Elisa quickly turned back on her heel without saying goodbye and headed back down the hall.

And I thought I was miserable.

I rolled my eyes and entered back into the room, not expecting the guy we had just been talking about to be sprawled out on one of the sofas as I did so.

I immediately jumped back with shock and as the door slammed closed, the guy lifted his head to look and his eyes popped open, gazing right in my direction. For a moment, we just froze, staring at each other, but because of my lack of movement, he soon loses interest and slumps his head back down and closes his eyes. I let out a quiet sigh of relief and began to walk back to my room, not wanting to be alone with this guy even if I didn't know if everything that I'd been told was true. After what I'd seen yesterday, I didn't want the chance of being electrified. However, just as I was halfway through the room, his voice suddenly rung in my ears.

"You! What is your name?" he suddenly blared from the couch, making me jump again.

I stood frozen for a moment, wondering when I had become such a coward, then built up the courage and went to sit in front of him on the velvet couches. "Why do you want to know?" I urged back, through a fake smug expression.

He narrowed his eyes, resting his head on his palm as he looked over to me. I just hoped I didn't look nervous; I felt slightly strange from the medicine that was still in my system and felt like all my weaknesses were showing at once.

"Just curious, I heard you are quite something."

"My name is Lexia and I heard you are a little crazy," I shot back.

"Well, nice to meet you, Lexia. My name is Xavier and to answer your very honest remark for being a stranger, the answer would be yes, I guess I am. However, aren't we all? This is a supernatural loony bin, after all."

I glared at his last words. "It's a training facility, not a loony bin, actually."

His face perked up at my sharpness. "Oh really, then how come everyone's here for strange reasons? Like Colt for example… You know him, right?" I nodded in reply before he continued, "He used his power to put thoughts into a girl's head to get her to like him, just so he could get laid but since his ability is useless, it failed, so she went insane. If that isn't the sign of a crazy person, I don't know what is."

"Well, that is very strange. However, that doesn't mean we are all crazy and I don't care about why other people are here anyway, I'm not here to know their business."

"Yes it does. You are crazy, because you blew up your college, correct?"

I gulped as he spat out the words. "I didn't know that was any business of yours, but how on earth did you find out?"

"So, it is true? Wow, you are a little fiery soul, eh?" He sat up and folded his legs, letting out a laugh.

"Shut up! How do you know? Isn't this against my privacy or something?!" I snapped.

"Don't worry, no one slipped the details. I was bored and had a root around Henry's office, learned quite the information about you. You are a Pyrokinetic too, right?"

His smugness was really starting to get to me, but the medicine in my veins didn't allow me to get to a high enough anger point to slap it away. "So what if I am?" I mutter.

"I've met plenty of supernaturals before. However, you are the first of that kind I have met. Therefore, I am mighty curious at just how strong you are, given you nearly blew up a whole building."

"Strong enough to light you up too if you look through my personal stuff again," I replied through narrowed eyes.

"Oh... I do like the feisty kind," he joked, before suddenly jumping up. "Anyway, I better get back. If I'm missing too long they'll make my sentence even longer. See you later, fire girl."

And with that he disappeared out the main entrance, smirking at me as he brushed past. I left him with my glare digging into his back, ignoring his remark for the last time. Maybe he was right, these people were nuts. It didn't matter though. I just had to focus on myself and ignore them. That way I could move forward and get out of here as quick as I could and start my new life. Though I had to remind myself to watch this guy, as there was something about his aura that made me feel uneasy.

Six

"That was so cool yesterday. You practically blew up the place," said Colt, seemingly amused by my spectacle yesterday, as we sat at the kitchen table early the next morning having breakfast. I sat at the table feeling no better than I had last night and I'd had zero sleep from the pain the medicine had left in my neck. When I pressed my palm onto the sore patch, it sent a burning pulse of pain down my spine.

I send him back an unimpressed look as I tried to bite back the agony I felt. "It's not funny," I grumbled. "I hate losing control like that."

"It was pretty cool though, I saw the heat radiating from your body like an atomic bomb. She is one to watch, everyone!" He wiggled his fingers around the table jokingly.

"Shut up," I urged through gritted teeth, digging into my bowl of cereal in annoyance. I was still full of anger after what happened yesterday and how I nearly lost control again. It seemed like every time more than just a ball of fire was about to explode from me, something cut me off and I passed out. I didn't know why that was. However, I knew one thing, I was getting annoyed with the whole situation and the quicker I learned to control this damned ability, the better. I let out a sigh as I had barely been here two days and already so much crazy stuff had happened.

Just as I was sulking about yesterday's event, Hunter suddenly came up and put a comforting arm around me. "Ignore him, Lexia. His power is so useless, he is amazed by anything."

As he spoke, his tone lingered with familiarity and I suddenly remembered what that strange electricity guy had told me last night.

"Yeah, how did you make that girl go insane?" I shot to Colt who seemed surprised by my question for a moment.

He slammed his hands on the table, the joking finger wiggles turning to claws. "I didn't make her go insane, she was already like that when I met her!" he yelled, before storming out the room with his toast.

"Bloody hell, someone is touchy," I said.

"Yeah, I always bring that up because I know it annoys him. However, I do wonder how you learned my trick, considering you just got here?"

I laughed. "That guy from last night told me about him."

"What guy?" Hunter enquired.

"Uh… Xavier, I think his name was."

Just as I was about to take a mouthful of cereal, Elisa suddenly slammed her magazine down on the table, almost making her glass of milk crash to the ground and nearly sending my cereal spilling all over me. "He was here?!" she screeched through gritted teeth.

I placed my now empty spoon back into my bowl. "Yeah, I came in here yesterday when you left and he was casually sprawled out on the sofa."

"What the heck, he got out again!" she yelled, knocking her magazine onto the floor as she left and became the second person of the day to storm out the room.

"Bloody hell, what was that?"

Hunter slid his arm away and sat in the seat facing me. "Xavier shouldn't have been here. He was supposed to be locked away, after what he had done to Elisa."

"Oh, yeah, forgot about that." I really had. After talking to him yesterday, the only thoughts about him I had were how much he annoyed me and how I hated the fact he knew why I was here.

"Are you okay?" I ask as Hunter's expression seemed to suddenly sour.

"Yeah, I'm fine," he half laughed before jumping up. "Anyway, you best get ready for today's training. Well, evaluation for you. Let's just hope they do it properly this time and start out lighter, eh?"

"What? After what happened yesterday I'm not going back there, are you crazy?"

"Don't worry, they won't make you do anything like that again. They fired those two idiots because they apparently put the whole company in jeopardy by pushing you too hard, even if it was a mistake. Anyway, you'll be put on a lighter evaluation, like you should have been to begin with."

My eyes widened. "Bloody hell, they were fired because of that? Well, so they should be I guess; I almost blew up the place."

And with that, I headed back to what would have been my true first day of training, had they not messed up my evaluation. I was taken to the same small room I had almost blown up previously, which they had managed to clean up pretty decently, considering the mess I had made. Being back here didn't sit well with me, however, I let them get on with it and gave them one last chance to prove themselves. The faster I got all this over with the better, as I could then finally start living a normal life.

Once I was inside, I was sat at a small table with nothing but a plate and piece of paper sitting in front of me. I was soon introduced to two new guards, a middle-aged plump woman named Rachel and a tall lanky man called Vincent. They looked friendly enough and as I got comfortable at the table, they went back outside and stood at the window facing me. The evaluation soon began.

"What I want you to do is simple, Lexia," said Rachel through the intercom. "Just like yesterday, only this time we have something for you to focus on. Focus all your energy onto the paper and set it alight. Only of course, don't go as huge as you did before. Would this be okay?"

I shrugged my shoulders. "Yeah, like I said yesterday, I'm fine with lighting small things—well sometimes, anyhow. Sometimes I can't focus on the object enough and it either doesn't catch fire or something else ignites instead."

"So, do you only pass out when you cause big explosions?" enquired Vincent, though I could hardly see his mouth move through his untamed greying moustache.

I nodded. "Yes, because the strength is too much for me. Though recently I haven't even touched my power because I was afraid I would cause an explosion even with the tiniest of flames. However, I soon found out that the more I hold it in, the worse it gets. That is how I lost control—I need to let it out once in a while, to let my veins breathe. Just not in big amounts, like I did yesterday. I don't know why my power works like that, it just does."

"I know, it was a mistake on our part as they accidentally put down on your training program that you were ready for a strong evaluation," Vincent smiled through his beard. "I'm sorry. Today, just use the smallest amount you can. Whatever is most comfortable for you."

"I'll try. I don't exactly want to use it, but I'm fine with small bouts given that I do know it helps. Just don't ever make me angry or stressed again like you did yesterday. That is why I went so insane, which is dangerous because it ignites the power. Okay?"

"We understand. Now, let's get started," said Rachel, before the click of the door soon locked me inside. "Now, when you are ready..."

"Wait, before we start, how exactly is this supposed to help me learn to control my ability?" I asked.

"It's not, yet. This is just to see exactly what power we are working with, as there are so many different types of abilities and strengths. Also, whether that person has control or not. We know it's Pyrokinesis but we like to see it in person first before we begin the actual control techniques, so we can assess the level to place you on. If this goes well, we shall begin with teaching you to be one with your power from tomorrow."

"I wish you'd done that yesterday, like you should have done," I grumbled through narrowed eyes.

"I know, I know, Lexia. Like I explained, it was a mistake on your program." I could tell they were starting to get frustrated with my constant reminders of yesterday. However, I wanted to make sure they never tested me so harshly again and made sure my program was labelled correctly from now on.

I soon let out a sigh and got myself comfortable in front of the piece of paper, giving the okay sign to them as I did so. I placed my hands up right against the oak table and closed my eyes for a few seconds as I calmed my body down. I let all negativity wash out of me and once I opened my eyes, I focused only on the object that was in front of me—the paper itself—and began to radiate my energy into it.

It was like building a thread connection piece by piece with the paper, as if my veins were connecting themselves to it and growing like roots, so I could directly aim my power to hit what I wanted. This didn't always work, however, as sometimes even the most minor of movements could distract me and a thread would break, meaning something else would catch fire alongside. However, I forged on and soon built a strong enough connection; sparks began to fray at the paper's edges. It continued to get brighter and brighter and eventually, the white shade was drowned away with the warmth of the orange glow.

"Well done, Lexia," Rachel said through the telecom. "How do you feel?"

"Okay, for now. But can we stop for a while?" I asked through a heavy exhale, as I felt myself getting tired already. I still hadn't recovered from using my power yesterday and the medicine still in my system wasn't helping.

Rachel ushered a hand for me to come through and after destabilising the connection I had made, I headed out back into the main area.

"You did a very good job there, Lexia," Vincent smiled on my way out.

"Good job. That is hardly a flame..." I sighed, as I looked back at the small fire I had made, which was as far as I could allow myself to go without losing control and beginning to blur out.

"Don't be so hard on yourself. You'll soon be able to control bigger fires soon enough, it just takes time. You have a very powerful gift inside you and since no one has helped you harness it, it will take a while to learn to live with it. However, practice makes perfect and from tomorrow we'll begin the proper training, okay?" Vincent smiled again and patted me on the shoulder before going to observe the flame, writing down notes on his clipboard before extinguishing it and coming back out.

"Yes, pyrokinesis is most definitely your ability," he laughed.

"Yeah, I thought that was obvious, given the reason I'm here," I replied unamused.

"We have to check in person so that we can give you the right treatment plan and get you on the right level," he smiled.

"Yes, I've heard this, for the thousandth time already. So, any clue what level I will be starting at?"

"Most likely level one, given you can only show a short burst of your power with control," interjected Rachel.

"Level one?!" I cried. "I know this place is supposed to help me but, there is like, twelve levels. I'll be here forever at this rate!"

"Lexia, you have had seventeen years of living without control. The process of gaining control won't happen overnight," Vincent said. And he was right.

I was most likely going to be here longer than I had imagined.

I let out one last sigh before turning back to the new staff member. "So, is that all today?"

"For now, yes. However, you can stay and observe the others if you like, get to know their abilities. Just don't disturb them if you do, alright?"

I gave a nod in response, having no intention of observing them as I had enough problems with my own power. However, as I was heading back to the dorm, I couldn't help but watch Hunter through the mirrored glass. He was standing in one of the booths, his face full of concentration as a member of staff guided him through the telecom on the other side. It weirdly made my heart flutter, seeing this guy in such a raw state as his face was so flustered and beads of sweat made his floppy brown hair stick to his forehead. I almost wanted to slap myself, given I had only just met the guy and was already admiring his appearance. It was so unlike me. I shook my head and focused more on what was starting to happen around him, which made my eyes widen slightly as the atmosphere changed.

A strange buzz began to fizzle around his body, as if his aura was beginning to burn with a transparent fire but it never quite got there. Parts of his body would disappear but he couldn't seem to manage it all and seconds later, it would reappear. This just seemed to make him get more annoyed as he kept kicking the wall after each failed spurt. I'd never seen someone's body disappear like that and all I guessed he could do was go invisible but obviously, given that we were here, he couldn't control it either.

Soon he seemingly gave up and began yelling in the booth. I couldn't hear what they were talking about, but judging by Hunter's expression, he was seriously frustrated. A few moments later he came out looking angry, storming past me and heading into the small waiting area. As I walked over, I heard a huge crash and he had kicked his foot into the side of the vending machine, leaving a huge dent as he leaned his head exhaustedly against the glass.

"Are you okay?" I enquired, even though I probably should have just left him be.

He whipped his head around to face me in surprise, before letting out a sigh and fixing his posture. "Yeah, I'm fine. Just tired," he said, before taking a seat on one of the couches. He ran a hand through his sweaty hair and let out an exhausted laugh. "Well, not really *fine*."

I went and sat down beside him and smiled. "I know what you mean. Annoying isn't it, the lack of control."

"You saw that then?"

I nodded. "You have a problem with control as well, huh?"

"We all do here. Sadly."

"I see. It's crazy, isn't it, how some of us supernaturals are born with control and others aren't."

"More like cruel," he urged, which for some reason made us both let out a laugh under our breaths. We both just sat there in silence for a moment after that, as I just left him to calm down.

"Well, I better get back to training," he suddenly said, jumping up from his seat. "You done for the day?"

"Yup," I sighed. "Early, once again. They said they were just observing my power officially today, so they can set me on the right course of treatment. Given that today went how it should have gone yesterday, I'm hoping *official* training begins tomorrow."

"Well, at least you are on the road to recovery now. Wish I could say the same for me. Anyhow, I'll see you back at the dorm later." And with that he headed back inside.

I stood there observing him for a few minutes, truly getting used to the sight of seeing another supernatural using an ability in front of me. It was actually quite comforting to see that I wasn't alone in this world in having such a useless power. Something I never thought I'd think. It wasn't just my father that was like this after all.

Seven

Before heading to the training area the next morning, I was greeted at the entrance by Miss. Ellewood, who escorted me away from the group and into a small room in another section of the facility. Inside were two men sitting at a desk in all black attire, not looking very approachable with their poker faces. But, then again, no one did here really.

Miss. Ellewood told me to sit facing them, as she sat at the side of the table rifling through a pile of papers and soon, Dr. Henry Lincoln entered and did the same. For some reason, as I sat there, I felt an odd vibe fill the room as they all shared short glances at each other. However, I brushed it off as Dr. Lincoln spoke up and I found out the reason I had been brought to this room.

"So, Lexia, how have you been settling in then?" he smiled, as he folded his hands casually onto the desk.

I shrugged my shoulders. "Apart from the mess-up the other day and seeing how weird this place is, I've been alright, I suppose. It's a very slow process indeed. Though I am generally just a very impatient person. Guess it's the fire in me," I said through narrowed eyes and straight away, I knew he could sense my annoyance.

"I understand that. And I'm very sorry about the other day, the mistake was on our part, it won't happen again I can assure you. I know it goes slow, but we just have to make sure we evaluate you correctly before you begin so we can put you on the right path. And with that said, after our colleagues looked at your results from yesterday's evaluation, we have your training treatment right here, which you will start as soon as this is over with."

"Really?" I smiled.

Dr. Lincoln nodded and pulled out a piece of paper from a black file on the table, soon sliding it over to me. "This is your treatment plan. I know I already gave you the times and everything else, however, this is your personalized plan. Where it shows what machines will be used and the level you will start at."

My expression soon dropped again, as I saw the level number printed plainly at the top of the page in bold. "So, I really have to start at level one then?" I grumbled.

"I'm afraid so. Your control is almost non-existent and with a power as strong as yours, we need to take the time with you. However, just think that when you leave here, the patience will have been worth it, as you will finally have learned to control the ability inside you."

"And I won't have to become like my dad," I interjected through a smile, as that thought alone was enough for me to continue. The one thing I wanted most, aside from gaining control of my pyrokinesis, was not to become like my dad. Who I was slowly turning into with my moody personality and hatred for everything. I knew that eventually, that would take over my mind just like it had his, and the fact that I had a chance of not becoming like him was enough of a reason for me to try hard.

"Yes, you won't be like your father," he smiled back.

I turned my gaze back to the paper and read through what treatments I would be doing. It had been really confusing me as to what they would be doing to help me gain control and now I was finally finding out as my eyes gazed over the words.

Monday and Tuesday: mind balance treatment.

Wednesday and Thursday: machine testing.

Fridays: in the testing rooms, where power will be used and changes examined.

"What exactly does all this mean?" I enquired, staring back up to Dr. Lincoln.

"Well, mind balance is where we take a small machine and attach it to the energy sources of your body with electrodes. This helps to lower the stress and anger brainwaves and so, sort of retrains your brain to listen to what you want to do and not just what it wants. Machine testing is basically brain games we play with you, to help zone in your focus. And the testing rooms are the booths you had your evaluation in, where you will use your power to begin to see if the previous tests are working." As he finished, I couldn't help but gulp as it felt like so much.

"Wow, that sure is a lot," I muttered, feeling suddenly overwhelmed.

"It may seem so, but it's all for the best. Just think, you'll soon have control over your power!"

"Let's hope," I said through a sigh, though still couldn't help but have doubts given my father and how long I had lived this way.

"Anyhow, I just wanted to tell you that your training begins today, so you can start to get ready for a new life ahead," he smiled again as he got up and shook my hand. "Be sure to let me know if you need anything, okay?"

I nodded back after shaking his hand and was soon thrown into my first official training day. I didn't know what to expect. I mean, I now obviously understood more of how things worked but still, I was hesitant. Also, given that my dad had once given up on this place, I wondered if I would too.

I was guided back to the training area by Miss. Ellewood, who soon disappeared and left me with a new staff member whom I had not seen before. Her name was Miri, a tanned and petite woman who coldly guided me to a space right at the back of the training area that led into another small section of rooms. I was placed into the farthest one from the door. Inside, there was nothing but a small white machine and a computer propped on a table top with a chair by its side.

"You just take a seat and we'll get started," Miri said. I followed the command and took a seat next to the odd machine.

"Is this the mind balance thing that Dr. Lincoln just told me about?"

"Yes, it's called an *Active Brain Wave Trainer*. We normally do this test on Mondays and Tuesdays, but since you started late and its now Tuesday, you will only get one session this week."

I gave a semi-understanding nod in response as she began to untangle the machine and place electrodes on all my energy points. Those being the temple, neck and main veins where my power would bleed out.

"Now, once this is switched on you will feel an odd sensation run through you. That is basically your electric impulses beginning to be re-tuned."

"Does it hurt?"

"It is uncomfortable, but not painful," she replied, but her cold tone doesn't send me any comfort. After fiddling with the machine some more and muttering a *get ready* under her breath, a button suddenly makes a loud *pop* and I begin to feel a prickling sensation start to radiate through my veins.

"Do you feel the pulses?" she enquired.

"I feel like constant pins and needles are running through my whole body and my head feels so light."

"It's working then. I'll be back in an hour to check on you."

"You're leaving me like this?!" I almost shrieked, not wanting to be alone with this odd machine.

"I have to. You need to be in utter silence for the machine to start to work on your brain."

"Oh, great, this should be fun." I sighed, but soon I was left to the silence of the space, which didn't actually last long before chaos unfolded in the institute.

We had to abruptly stop after some sudden explosion shook somewhere in the building and the day was cancelled. After Miri untangled me from the machine, I was rushed out of the training area with the others and back to the dorms.

I couldn't believe something else had happened again to ruin the day, even though this time it wasn't me. As I was walking back to the dorm, I was raging with anger as I was actually getting annoyed at the fact I had already hit day two and things weren't progressing. However, I reminded myself it was either this, jail or a coffin.

As our group got back to the dorm, I immediately went and lay down on one of the sofas, already exhausted even though I hadn't done much.

"I'm so tired," I croaked.

"Me too..." said Colt, slumping next to me. "They tried to make me put a curse on a tomato, of all things."

"Yeah, well, I had to sit in silence for almost an hour while attached to a machine so I wonder whose day was weirder. Sadly, we were interrupted again so I barely did anything," I stated, letting out a sigh.

"Crazy things happen all the time here, better get used to it. Hey, anyhow, I never did ask what your powers were. I mean, I sorta seen them but I have no idea what it is called?" Colt suddenly enquired and I instantly felt everybody's gaze dig into me.

I narrowed my eyes and let out a sigh. "Does it matter?"

"Well, we all know each other's, might as well join in!"

"What are yours then? Pervert power?" I shot to Colt, whose

voice was beginning to annoy me.

Everyone laughed around him. "Actually, I can put curses on people!" he said proudly.

"Yeah, they are curses alright..." added Hunter.

"Well, why don't you tell her what you can do, Mr. Superior? Oh and the reason you are here..."

Hunter shot him a cold glare. "I will happily tell her." He turned his eyes to me and even though I had seen him use his ability the other day, I still didn't truly know what he could do. "I can teleport," he finished.

My eyebrows raised, impressed. "Wow, how cool."

"That's cool? More like boring," muttered Colt.

"At least I don't have to put a curse on a girl to like me," said Hunter through a gallant smile.

"I told you, I didn't!" Colt shouted back, digging his nails into the edge of the sofa.

Hunter rolled his eyes and turned his gaze to Elisa. "Why don't you tell her what you can do?"

"Why?" she replied, bored, before rolling her eyes and finally continuing, "I can talk to the dead and even raise them, okay."

"You're a necromancer?" I replied with a raised brow.

She shook her head. "Ew, don't ever mention that word in front of me. No, I'm not."

"Oh, come on, forget about them," Colt interrupted. "We all want to know what you can do!"

I rolled my eyes before unleashing the word. "Pyrokinesis."

"I see, that is how you nearly set the place up in flames yesterday then," Elisa said.

"Yes, that was their fault, not mine. They made a damn mistake on my plan. They know the reason I'm here is because I blew up my college when this girl wouldn't just leave me alone and..." I soon trailed off when I realised I had said too much.

"You blew up your college? Sweet!" said Colt, whose eyes gleamed with a sudden curiosity.

"No, it wasn't *sweet*," I shot back.

"Did anyone die?" All eyes turned to me as Colt asked the question.

"Uh... well. Yeah, there were some casualties, but only those who aggravated me."

"And I thought what I had done was bad..." Colt suddenly

murmured.

"So, you admit it, you're a pervert then!" shouted Hunter, suddenly pointing his finger at Colt, his face full of mischief and I almost wanted to hug him for taking the spotlight off me.

"Shut up, I never said that!" cried Colt red-faced, before storming out the room as usual.

"Well, as fun as this discussion is, I'm going too. Nice to know we have another freak in here anyway. Though you certainly top the pile of weirdos since we have never had a murderer here before. Well done," Elisa said steaming out the room, my glare digging into her back as she did so.

"Bloody hell, talk about miserable," I muttered.

"Don't mind her," said Hunter, moving to sit next to me. "She's just sour in general. She can continuously hear the dead speak to her so she turned out this way."

My brows raised. "Wow, that must be a pain."

"Yeah, I guess. Anyway, I have just realised you haven't been given the grand tour of the facility, have you?"

I shook my head in response. "Well, I've seen everything in here, if that is what you mean?" I said, motioning around the common area of the dorm.

"No," he said, shaking his head. "The whole place outside of here, want to take a look? I have to warn you though, we have to sneak out in order for you to see. You up for it?"

I shrugged my shoulders as I had nothing else to do. "Sure, why not? But, how are we going to get out of here anyway."

I soon wanted to kick myself for asking that.

"Teleportation, of course, my dear Lexia." Suddenly he jumped up and placed out his hand towards me. "You ready to travel through thin air?" he added through a smile that almost made me blush.

"I thought you couldn't control it?"

"I can't. However, short trips are *mostly* fine when I'm not stressed."

After a moment of debating with myself, I shrugged my shoulders and jumped up beside him. "Sure, why not?" And as soon as I placed my hand in his, we vanished out the room through my first ever teleportation experience.

Eight

My whole body planted face first into the ground as we landed in one of the white halls I had entered through. I almost passed out in the process of having my first ever teleportation experience and it was not at all pleasant.

"You could have told me that would happen," I grumbled to Hunter, as I clutched my bruised forehead and a sickening feeling churned inside of my stomach from how fast we had rushed through whatever dimension that was.

"Sorry, I don't often travel with other people, I forgot how tricky it can be," Hunter joked while putting out a hand to help me up.

I gave him a bemused glare as I stumbled back up, glancing around the space we had landed in. There was nothing but a long stretch of corridors greeting us at either end.

"Do you often do this, teleport out of base?" I enquired, wondering what there was to see.

"Yeah," he smiled back, gazing around each end to seemingly make sure no one was about.

"Why, what else is here that is worth venturing out of base for?"

"You'll soon see, but first I need to go to the vending machine," he replied, my face scrunching up in confusion at his odd interjection.

"Well, that was random," I said confused.

"Trust me, it keeps him happy," he said with raised brows and a slight playful smile curling at his lip.

"Him? Who exactly is that?" My eyebrows raising too out of curiosity, as we began to trek down the corridor to the left of where we had landed.

"You'll see soon enough," Hunter repeated, while he glanced

through the small circular window on the steel door that was laying at the end of the hall. At the all clear, to my surprise, as he placed his palm on the handle, it opened without force.

We peeked our heads through the door. A small empty seating area with a vending machine tucked away in the corner greeted us and we hurriedly headed over. Letting Hunter take the lead since I had no idea who this person was we were going to visit and why this vending machine seemed so important.

I let out a sigh as we stood there, annoyed at the fact I had left the base to come and steal some candy bars and visit a stranger. "I thought you were showing me around?" I urged in annoyance.

"I am, sort of. Well, to one place anyway." He suddenly punched onto the side of the vending machine and out fell three candy bars. "Now, let's teleport again."

I could feel my face pale over as he said that, my stomach still feeling sickly. "What, do we have to?"

However, before I could reject it, he grabbed me by the wrist and we disappeared once again, landing with a crash on the floor seconds later, only this time facing upwards.

I lay there for a moment letting my eyes adjust to the room, as it seemed to want to spin around. "You really need to work on that landing," I grumbled as I stumbled up, the room eventually clearing into an unknown space.

Just as I was about to gaze around to try and work out where we were, a voice suddenly chirped up.

"Finally," said a familiar deep tone from the background and as I turned my head, recognition dawned on me as the guy from yesterday–Xavier if I recalled— gazed glumly at Hunter.

"What took you so long?" Xavier moaned, stomping over and grabbing a bar from Hunter's grasp before slumping back down on a hospital-style metal bed. That was strangely the only piece of furniture situated in the small pale room.

Hunter let out a sigh and leaned his back against the wall facing the bed, unsealing the side of the candy bar before taking a bite. "I've been in bloody training that is what. I would have been later if there hadn't been an explosion."

Xavier laughed while he took a bite from the chocolate. "Yeah, I got bored earlier."

Hunter just let out another exhausted sigh. "You'll never get out of here if you keep doing that, you know."

"You!" I shouted suddenly at Xavier, breaking off their conversation. "What are you doing here?"

Xavier's eyes lazily turned to me. "I live here, like you. What else?" he replied bluntly.

I narrowed my gaze and turned to Hunter. "What are *we* doing here, with this guy?"

Hunter's gaze widened a little, seemingly surprised by my question. "I came to see my brother." As he finished the sentence, I couldn't help but stand there in confusion at his words.

"You're *brothers*?" They both simply nodded in chorus. "But, you are so—"

"*Different*?" said Hunter. "I'm peppy and he is annoying? I'm the good-looking one and he—"

"Hey," interjected Xavier. "Correct yourself, I'm the good-looking one."

I bit my lip so as not to laugh, as I didn't want to show my amusement when I was annoyed to be in the same room as this guy. I had to admit though, they actually were both good-looking and as I had only known them for such a short time, I hadn't truly observed their appearances so much. Although at first glance you couldn't really tell they were brothers, now I saw them together, the similarities were easier to spot.

They both had dark hair, except Xavier's lay in a mop of short black curls untamed around his face, the spikes now deflated from when I had first seen him trying to electrify Elisa. And Hunter's was slicked back into a rather sleek quiff. Both of them had different eye colours though—Xavier's were a pure blue shade and Hunter's were hazel. Their skin both glowed with a sun-kissed sheen.

I cleared my throat and looked away so as not to show I was actually, observing them. "Yeah, anyway, why didn't you tell me he was your brother?" I said.

Hunter shrugged his shoulders. "It never really crossed my mind, I suppose it's because you haven't been here long."

I gave an understanding nod in response but couldn't help feeling slightly upset that this cool and charming guy had such an annoying and arrogant brother. And even though I hadn't truly talked much to Xavier, by first impressions, I already couldn't stand him.

"Anyhow, I don't understand why you teleported here. I was talking to Xavier in the dorm yesterday, wouldn't have just meeting there saved this trouble?"

Hunter laughed and tilted his head towards Xavier. "You really need to stop wandering around while you are under probation, Xavier. We'll end up being here forever." Xavier just smirked back as Hunter continued and turned his gaze to me, "He's not supposed to leave this room, which he keeps doing. But of all places, why did you go back to the dorm, you idiot?"

Xavier shrugged his shoulders, chucking his chocolate bar wrapper onto the floor. "Well, I knew you would all be in training so I decided to go back and watch some television. It's bloody boring in here you know."

Hunter's eyes gleamed with sudden curiosity. "So, what did you guys exactly talk about yesterday then?"

"Nothing of interest," I replied plainly, folding my arms.

"Oh, quite the contrary. She learned that this place is for the insane sorts of supernaturals. The unwanted wayward youth of society," he put on a weird mocking tone as he said the last part.

I narrowed my gaze, unamused. "Yes, maybe you can apply that fact to yourself but I'm perfectly sane."

"Yes, it's perfectly sane to blow up a college, isn't it?" he smirked back, which was beginning to truly aggravate me, something this strange guy seemed to be a master of.

My face pulled into a scowl. "Bloody hell, shut up about that!"

"I can't," he said, placing his hand to his heart. "Not until you see you are just as crazy as the rest of us, fire girl."

A muscle in my jaw twitched as he stared back at me full of amusement but I ignored his taunts. "Stop with the fire girl," is all I muttered back.

"Anyway, at least the introductions are done," said Hunter, trying to break the awkwardness.

After a few more silent moments, we eventually got talking and spent the next hour in the room with Xavier before eventually having to make a quick exit. As we heard footsteps rise from outside of the door and Xavier informed us his stripper had arrived. In fact, his tests were just about to begin. I shot him an unamused glare.

Just as we were about to teleport away, he left me with a message that I had just told him not to say to me: "Nice seeing you again, fire girl."

And just as I was about to shoot back a profanity, we disappeared out the room.

Nine

After having been acquainted with Xavier again, I soon began to realise he was the type of person that could easily exhaust you just through words. The fact I had now found out that he was brothers with such a cool guy like Hunter made no sense to me, but sadly, I had to accept it.

Hunter teleported us into the dorm cubicle and after I landed with another face plant with the ground, we suddenly heard a raised discussion coming from the main lounge. As we entered, we saw Elisa flailing around the common area with excitement, her face for the first time not scrunched up like she had just sucked a lemon.

"I can't believe this, are you serious?" she said.

I looked up to see who she was shrieking to, and saw Dr. Lincoln standing in front of her with a smile. He was in his usual white lab coat and his greying untamed hair lay casually against his aged skin.

"Of course I am serious, Elisa," he smiled while patting her on the shoulder. "We have been so impressed with your progress and in such a short span of time too. We are happy to tell you that you can finally start to get ready to head home."

"What is going on?" I asked Colt, who was sitting on the edge of the sofa looking rather glum.

He didn't take his glare away from Lincoln as he responded. "They are letting her go home, it's so unfair," he pouted, before suddenly jumping up and barging in front of Elisa. "This is ridiculous, she has only been here a month and I have been here for four. How can she go home and I can't?!" Colt yelled to Dr. Lincoln, whose wrinkled face remained calm.

Elisa let out a sarcastic laugh in the background and put her hands on her hips as she glared at Colt. "Because I have gained control and you haven't. You're useless, that is why; too busy wondering who will be your next pervy victim."

Colt scoffed back. "No, you haven't! You have the worst control here—even worse than Lexia, who nearly blew up the place. And shut up saying stuff like that!"

"Well, thanks..." I murmured under my breath, knowing he had a point though.

"Oh, get over yourself, Colt. It's not my fault you are rubbish at this," she shot back proudly.

Before Colt could sulk anymore, Dr. Lincoln interjected, "Look, we evaluate you all equally. I'm sorry you feel that way, Colt. However, I'm afraid this is just the way it goes. It doesn't matter how long you have been here, it's all based on how you progress."

Colt did his usual routine and stormed out of the room.

"I can't help it if he's rubbish at this! No need to take it out on me," Elisa said, her smile soon curling at her lips again as she turned back to Dr. Lincoln. "I still can't believe it!"

As Elisa was boasting away to anyone that would listen to her, Hunter suddenly let out a sigh and walked into the kitchen, slouching down on a seat. I followed him inside, curious to his sudden shift in mood; as he laid his head on his palm and then suddenly punched the side of the table.

"Are you okay?" I said.

He shrugged his shoulders as he leaned back in the chair. "I'm just sick of this place. I've been here for almost a year, you know? Yet still, here I am. It's a bloody joke she is getting to leave that early."

My eyebrows raised in surprise and at the same time, the prospect of staying here for a year made me feel uneasy, as it was a thought I couldn't bear. "You've been here a year?"

He nodded. "Yeah, well, I know it was my doing. However, what annoys me most is my brother being here—it was all my stupid fault and yet he is getting the worst of it."

"What do you mean?"

"Xavier didn't really do anything to warrant being here, he was just protecting me and because of that, he is here as well. It should just be me. The fact he is locked away in that room because of me makes me feel like the worst brother in the world."

"What did he exactly do?" I enquire curiously.

"Well, nothing but protect me really. He has better control over his power, however, these people will never see that. Basically, I went to rob a bank, which is a long story. Anyhow, when I teleported us out of the bank space, it was accidentally right in front of the police, as I lost control. To escape, he was going to use his power to blow everything up." Hunter ran a hand through his hair and let out a sigh. "And, well .... he did just that."

My eyebrows raised. "What, he blew them up, the police?" Hunter nodded. "Why didn't you just teleport quickly away from them?" I pressed.

Hunter shrugged his shoulders. "Because like I said, I've never had good control of my power and as I landed there, I panicked, so Xavier felt like he had no choice but to do it. It was all my fault."

"What did you do when he blew them up?"

"We were just about to run away. However, that is when *they* showed up in front of us and it was all too late."

"*They* meaning Lucida?"

He nodded. "Yeah, they have been on our backs for a while now, trying to capture us. And before I could even try to teleport again, they had already shot us with those drug things and we passed out. We ended up here and had to stay, as they said it was either here or some supernatural jail. Since it wasn't the first time we had done this type of thing... I won't go into that."

I couldn't help but let out a half-hearted laugh. "They threatened me too. Well, sort of."

His eyes gleamed as he looked up at me. "Really? Why is that?"

"Well, I..." I trailed off, not truly wanting to bring up the past again.

"Oh yeah, you blew up your college, didn't you. What happened exactly?"

I shrugged my shoulders. "Well..." I gritted my teeth and decided to just spit the words out. "It was just an accident. I was trying to get out of the college because I knew I was going to lose it, but this damn girl wouldn't leave me alone, so I lost control of my power and everything just started to explode around me. I've never lost control like that before. Not to that extent anyhow." I let out a sigh at the memory. "I wouldn't stay here either to be honest, but like you said, it's either here or a life of more destruction for me. Anyhow, I don't want to become like my dad, who ultimately killed himself because he couldn't bear his ability anymore, I decided to just brave it out. Mainly because my aunt really wanted me to try and get control of my abilities once and for all but also because I know I need to. Anyhow, they threatened to lock me away in the supernatural prison thing like you, which was the other major reason I came here, I guess."

"Wow, sorry to hear about your dad."

I shrugged my shoulders. "It's fine, as bad as it may sound, I don't miss him. He was a drunk and used to beat me to take the edge off the pain of his power amongst other reasons."

We stayed silent for a minute as my words lingered in the air before he finally let out a sigh.

"So, looks like we are both here for strange reasons." Hunter exclaimed through a long exhale.

"Anyhow, I wouldn't worry so much about your brother, you know. He was just protecting you, I would have done the same for my sibling, if I had one. You can't feel guilty just because your power faulted."

Hunter sat back casually in his chair and a smile curled at the corner of his lip. "I guess you're right. It's just not easy, you know. Though you must be close to your aunt too, given you would come here."

"Well, I don't exactly have a choice nor is it just for her. However, she is the main reason Lucida know about what happened, as she called them when the incident occurred. However, I have nothing against her, she just wants to help me. That's why I haven't run away, as I know I need help. Anyway, let's not fret on the past. How about we work together from here forth to try and get control of our powers?"

"I've been here a year and still don't have full control, what could we possibly do?"

"That's just because the people who are training us have no idea what it is like to have an uncontrollable power. We both know the struggles of what it is like, so what do you say?" I put out my hand and surprisingly, he immediately shook it.

"You're right, we can probably help each other so much better. Let's do it and hopefully it will help us to get the hell out of here faster."

I smiled. "That is the spirit!"

Sitting here with Hunter and getting to know each other slowly made me feel so much more content that for the first time in a long while, I had the hopes of making a friend that I actually didn't mind.

And sharing what happened to me with someone who understood my viewpoint and didn't instantly think of me as crazy, like Xavier seemed to think, made me feel like a weight was lifted off my shoulders and that I could finally, slowly, start to get my life back on track. I just hoped that from here forth, everything would just work out, for once in my life.

Ten

The first two weeks at the facility went faster than I had imagined they would, which was a very nice surprise indeed. Hunter and I continued to build a strong bond as we learned more about each other too. From our similar lives of growing up in broken homes to our evidently terrible control of our abilities and how we hoped to finally just become normal people in society when we left here.

Everything was going somewhat well. However, sadly, in that time the progress of my abilities didn't gain that much speed. And after Elisa left about a week after I had arrived, the atmosphere in the place seemed to change drastically. Even though I had hardly spoken to her nor did I like her very much, it was sad that I was now going to be the only girl in the dorm. Also, Colt, despite their arguments, seemed to oddly miss her taunts and so became more argumentative as the days passed, which was very annoying.

However, three weeks after Elisa left, that all changed as a surprise new guest—not Xavier, who had continued to annoy me whenever he escaped his asylum—arrived in the place and took over an empty slot. Her name was Dana Sukimoto. A black-haired, doe-eyed, pale girl who at first acquaintance seemed like a normal enough person. However, after a week of her being there, we soon realised that was far from the truth.

An odd normality had begun to take us over as we got used to Elisa not being around. This was soon discarded when we were woken up one morning by Colt's screams for help coming out of the common area and as we all stumbled out of our rooms groggily, saw him cowering in the corner near the blocked-out windows, looking as if he had just seen a ghost. And sadly, from here forth, everything that would forge ahead just began to bite away at the smooth path that had been going on since I had arrived. We were sent into a never-ending mix of disaster.

"What the hell is all this commotion?" demanded Hunter through a tired gaze.

Colt looked at us while shaking, his blue and white flannel pajamas clinging to his body with sweat.

"It's her!" Colt shouted through a shaky tone. "She came into my room and jumped on me!"

"Her, who?" groaned Hunter.

"The new girl, Dana!"

Hunter rolled his eyes and laughed "I thought you would have enjoyed that?"

"Not when she began taking my energy away, I didn't!"

"Your energy?" I said out of confusion.

"Yeah, she tried to kill me. Felt like she was sucking out my soul!"

Me and Hunter exchanged odd glances, when suddenly Dana walked into the room, seemingly as bewildered as us as to what was happening.

"What is going on?" she blurted, rubbing at her eyes.

"Apparently, you just tried to kill Colt?" Hunter said.

She stood there unfazed by the accusation. "Oh... Sorry. That would have been the other me. I did warn the guards she can come out from time to time."

We all stood there wide-mouthed at her response. "What are you talking about, *the other me*?" Colt said.

"Well, that is why I am here. To learn to control her—the darker side of me. I thought you all would have known?"

We all shook our heads.

"Why did she attack me?!" Colt spouted.

"She must have been hungry. She feeds on energy, sometimes blood. Though don't worry, it shouldn't happen again," Dana finished, before turning back and heading to her room as if this all seemed so normal.

"Is she serious?" I exclaimed.

Hunter scratched his head. "Seemingly so. I don't care anyhow, it's way too early to be talking about rubbish like this. I'm going back to sleep."

As Hunter and I headed back to our rooms, Colt shouted from behind, "You can't just leave me here. She just tried to attack me!"

"Then stay in here or lock yourself in the bathroom, I don't care," Hunter stated as we left him to cower in the corner.

A few hours later, we all woke to see Colt still curled in a ball in the corner of the common room, fast asleep.

"Whoa, didn't think she would scare him that much," said Dana plainly. "Guess it wasn't a dream then."

I rolled my eyes, too exhausted to deal with this after being interrupted at such an early time, and walked myself over to the table, not even wanting to dig into the toast Hunter had placed in front of me.

"You okay?" he enquired, sitting beside me and taking a gulp of his tea.

"I'm just a little tired..." I replied, giving Dana a glare.

"Don't look at me, I can't control her," she mumbled through a mouthful of cereal.

Hunter and I gave a wide-eyed gaze to each other.

For the rest of the day, a strange feeling couldn't help but linger inside me. I couldn't quite put my finger on what it was and it wasn't the fault of what had happened this morning or the tiredness; it was like a sense of dread, but I just couldn't understand why I felt that way.

I shook off the feeling as much as I could as we had training, but for some reason as the day panned out, it just got worse.

"Lexia, it's the third time in a row now you've failed this test, we really need your full concentration," groaned Miri while I was in training, sitting with electrodes glued to my body as I sleepily gazed into the machine ahead of me.

"I'm sorry, I'm just not in the right frame of mind," I mumbled.

"Look, let's take a break and try again in a short while, okay. Get your bearings."

I gave a nod in response, before I stumbled over to the waiting room and stood by the vending machine to rest a moment.

"What's wrong with me today..." I muttered under my breath.

My head felt so clouded and heavy; it was like a mist was floating in on a cold day and I just couldn't see past it. The only possible word I could think to describe the feeling was a hangover, magnified by one-hundred. And as the time passed, I realised something was seriously wrong, because my eyes began to completely glaze over and my body felt as if all the energy had been drained from it.

That was when all of a sudden it became too much. The misty haze that had surrounded my vision now started to fade away everything in front of me and slowly my body gave way and I went crashing to the floor. Even though the blackout was a momentary blip, my head still felt like I had just fought someone and been sucker-punched in the face.

A few moments later, as I lay exhausted on the floor, I felt a presence beside me. Then there was a gasp that was accompanied by a familiar yet worried voice calling my name.

"Lexia, what is going on?" Hunter's voice said, panic-stricken.

I lazily shrugged my shoulders as he managed to pull me back up to the sofa, while calling for help at the same time.

"I don't know, I just feel rotten all of a sudden..." I mumbled.

"You look terrible, all the colour has drained from your face," he said, pushing back my hair before I heard a low tone coming from the doorway.

"Oh no, I didn't mean for this to happen," cried Colt suddenly as he stood in the doorway. As I faced him, my eyes managed to adjust enough to see his face blanch over with fear.

Hunter whipped his head around. "What are you going on about?"

Colt bit at his lip, tugging nervously at his red flannel shirt. "Well, after what happened this morning and you all just left me there, I sort of got angry and put a tiny curse on Lexia..."

"You tried to put a curse on me? What for?!" I yelled, my head still feeling foggy, but as a sudden gush of anger ran through me it gave me a bout of energy enough to shout.

"I'm sorry, alright. I was just angry about how you two ignored me earlier!"

Hunter suddenly jumped up and pushed Colt against the wall, grabbing him by the neck.

"I said I'm sorry! I just wanted to get back at you for not giving a damn about me! I thought we were friends!" cried Colt.

Hunter's grip around his neck tightened. "What the hell did you want me to do? I'm not a bloody magician. I can't make her stop using her power!"

"It was an accident, I didn't mean to! Like you all, I can't control my powers sometimes, especially when I'm angry!"

"There has been plenty of times I've been angry with you, but I never lost control of my power, you damn idiot! What have you done to me anyway?" I urged.

"I just put a darkening curse on you is all."

"What does that mean?"

"Well, not much. It's supposed to make you feel like crying all the time. However, I got it wrong, as you aren't meant to pass out."

"I'm gonna kill you!" I spat and went to lunge for his throat, but with my body now feeling so weak, I could barely move.

"Woah, chill," Hunter said, while turning to Dana who suddenly appeared at the door. "Dana, go and get the guards to take this damn cretin away before this escalates."

"This was your fault anyway, you shouldn't have ignored me!" Colt said and I soon realised how much he loved attention and would do anything for it.

"Then why didn't you put the spell on me!" Hunter spat.

"Because I knew by putting it on her it would get to you more!"

Just before Hunter was about to lunge for Colt himself, the guards arrived and we explained what had happened. Hunter soon dropped Colt to the floor and as he was taken away, I couldn't help but sigh with relief, as at least I would get a break from him for a while. I mean, it's not like he was normally a bad guy, but he never stopped talking and often clung to me at any chance he could get, which I knew I wouldn't be letting him get away with anymore.

The moment of relief I felt soon melted away, as I heard a familiar voice come crashing through the doors and into the waiting space.

"I'm back, you crazy people!" Xavier beamed and the sense of dread slowly seeped back into me. He barged into the room, all guns blazing, our gazes meeting instantly and his familiar mischievous expression soon turning up.

"Hey my little fiery soul, we finally get to be roommates, eh?" he said, while walking past me to Hunter and wrapping an arm around his shoulder. "It's good to be back," he stated.

I couldn't help but let out a sigh as I realised I was back to square one with my emotions. The normality that had formed had just been swept away in one smooth hit and I just knew this was going to be one long stretch with him around full time.

Eleven

The arrival of Xavier did nothing but render me with annoyance and alongside having him around, I had to live for three days with the messed-up curse Colt had put on me. Three days of headaches, bouts of crying for no reason and nausea.

Xavier also didn't officially enter back into the main facility until two days after his reappearance and as soon as he did, he made sure his presence was known. As I was sitting on the couch trying to read up on my powers one day, still trying to recover from the after-effects of the curse, Xavier slumped on the sofa in front of me, determined to annoy me at every given chance he could get. And now he no longer had to sneak out of his locked room, he could irritate me so much more, which he seemed to enjoy way too much.

"Hey, my little fire soul, happy to see me?" he beamed, mischief glazed over his face.

I rolled my eyes, returning them quickly to the pages of my book, which I wasn't now truly reading as I could feel his gaze on me. "Yes, delighted," I lied.

"Good to know," he said, suddenly jumping up and slipping down into the seat next to me. "So, what you reading?"

"*The History of Pyrokinesis.*"

"Trying to brush up on your abilities, eh? I wouldn't bother reading those then," he urged, flicking the side of my book. "They are written by a bunch of lying old normal folk, who have no idea what it's like to live with actual abilities."

I let out a soft sigh. "Then you don't have to. Leave me alone and annoy someone else, will you."

"Why would I, when you are so fun to taunt?" A grin crept up at the corner of his lip. After I didn't reply, he let out a soft laugh.

"Don't you want to know what my power is?" he said whispering in my ear. I almost turned to punch him but he stood up too quickly.

"I didn't know I gave off the vibes I cared," I stated bluntly, even though I already somewhat knew.

"Look," he said, before a sudden familiar light blue bolt erupted from his hand and hit the back of Dana as she walked across to the kitchen, causing her to emit an almighty yelp.

"What was that?!" she yelled, rubbing her singed neck.

Xavier just shrugged his shoulders in response. "I think you are giving off electric vibes Dana, better get that checked."

Dana just glared at him before going into the kitchen.

"I could get you removed for that," I urged.

"I'd like to see you try," he replied, leaning suddenly close to my face.

"What is going on here?" Hunter suddenly said, entering the room and breaking away our awkward gaze.

My face suddenly blistered with redness as I whipped my head away. "Uh, could you please tame your brother, Hunter?" I jumped up and tried to divert the arising situation.

"Come on," Hunter said, dragging Xavier away to the kitchen.

I could finally sigh with relief. Though knowing he was going to be like this and he was staying here, I couldn't help but let out an added sigh of exhaustion alongside.

After the morning of annoyance, we headed to another day of training, now with Xavier tagging along by our side. It was another day that didn't go smoothly with another person seemingly losing control of their powers once again, to an extreme extent. This time around it was not me, surprisingly, but Dana.

It happened just as I was trying to focus on making a flame grow larger. We heard a sudden crashing in the room Dana was practicing in, followed by an almighty shout for help. All the staff immediately jumped up and swung open the door, only to find Dana casually gnawing away into her supervisor's neck, blood smeared all over her face as she turned up her head to us.

"Damn, she a vampire or something?" Xavier said, his face scrunching up as he gazed repulsively at the bloody scene.

"She has two sides to her apparently—one crazier than the other," Hunter replied, looking just as freaked out by the image.

I walked over to gaze closer at the spectacle, I saw them trying to tackle the crazy side of Dana to the ground, before eventually stabbing her in the neck with a shot.

"Bloody hell, if things like this keep happening, I'm never going to be able to train and get out of here," I stated in anger.

"Are any of us?" replied Hunter with a sigh. "Where will she be taken?" he enquired, as two guards in white lab coats and masks carried her now limp body out of the room.

"To a secure unit while she calms down. I always said she was too dangerous to place in the main facility. I think we will most likely be bringing in some new, less disturbed recruits. So, prepare yourself for a new inmate or two, I'd imagine," one of the guards said flustered, before dragging the now lifeless body of Dana away, never to be seen again.

"More idiots, just what we need," stated Xavier in his usual blunt manner, as he turned on his heel and headed towards the vending machine.

"Well, back down to just three of us," I muttered under my breath. The three of us still just being me, Hunter and Xavier, since Colt was still locked away. I just wished that crazy things would stop happening and I could actually learn something.

Xavier's face suddenly beamed with a mischievous look as I turned and bumped right into him, making a frown crease at my forehead as he was way too excited after what had just happened.

"Hey Lexi," he smirked, suddenly placing his hands on my shoulders. "I've just thought, now the facility will probably be quiet for a while, that means we pretty much have the place to ourselves. Ignoring my brother." He moved his mouth to my ear, lightening his tone. "Now we've got the space to ourselves, how about you and I finally get it on? Ouch!" Before he could finish, I kicked him in the shin and threw his arms off me, storming out the room with a smile on my face as I had finally vented some anger upon him.

However, as I walked away back to the dorm with Xavier's shouts lingering in the background, I knew the session wouldn't be resuming today after what happened. My frustration soon poured back, as I couldn't help but wonder if I would ever be able to train without being disturbed. Something, now three weeks in, that seemed like an impossible ideology and couldn't help but make me wonder if this place was here to help us at all.

Twelve

A week after the spectacle in the training room, Dana was truly never to be seen again, in our part of the facility anyhow. The guards had informed us she was being taken care of somewhere else in the main headquarters and so, with her loss, we were soon presented with a new inmate, as well as Colt, who was now back from isolation and made sure to keep his distance from me, as I gave him a death glare as he entered. Dr. Lincoln had also accompanied the new roommate and decided to have a talk to us all, as the situation over the past few weeks had been a little chaotic to say the least.

"I've hardly done any training," I complained to him as we all sat at the sofas that evening. "Something crazy happens every other day. I'll never get out of here at this rate."

He cleared his throat before speaking, and held an expression to me that looked like he was sick of hearing my complaints. "I understand your concern Lexia and it is a fair one at that. You must have a bad first impression of the place, as you seemed to have arrived at such an awkward time. However, I assure you, we never normally run this way, it's just a lot has been going on and we have not had enough time to supervise everything." He cleared his throat again before continuing, "Now, just think of the arrival of your new roommate as a fresh start and from today, we will proceed in a new light."

Dr. Lincoln shuffled over to our new housemate and smiled. "Anyhow, I'm in a bit of a rush, so I will have to trust you all to get acquainted," he said, before patting me awkwardly on the shoulder and leaving us in the room.

As everyone sat there awkwardly gawking at the new arrival, no one seemed to want to speak up first, so I rolled my eyes and edged in some words to break the tension.

"Why don't you sit down?" I urged the guy, who seemingly followed the order and perched himself on the sofa in front of our curious eyes.

"So, what are you here for?" enquired Xavier.

"Shut up, Xavier. It's none of your business," I said.

He shrugged his shoulders. "What? If we have to share this place with people, we should all know what we are capable of."

"Why don't you introduce yourself?" I urged, brushing his rudeness off.

As he looked up at me through his spectacles, brown eyes widening at me creepily, I felt an odd vibe radiate from him as our gazes met.

"I'm Ben Ronson," Ben said in a soft voice, with the most quintessentially English accent I had heard. Which oddly seemed to match his lanky and thin character well.

I brushed off the odd feeling for now and smiled. "Nice to meet you," I replied.

"So, where are you from?" Hunter said.

"I'm from Kensington, London. I shouldn't be here though, you know," said Ben, as he looked down at the floor, seeming as if he was trying to hold back tears.

"I know how that feels, I shouldn't be in this place either," I sympathized and sent a glare in Xavier's direction as I did so, as just the thought of being here for the same type of reasoning as him just made my stomach churn. "I'm Lexia Luccen, by the way. I'm from Newcastle, so a long way from you—"

"What are you here for, if you don't mind me asking?" enquired Hunter, somewhat cutting me off.

Ben let out a soft sigh. "I kind of lost control once and hurt a girl. It was an accident though... Anyway, I can sort of control people's minds, often by accident."

"Mind manipulation? Bet that is fun to play with," I state, imagining all the people I could tell what to do and the situations I could get out of.

He shrugged his shoulders, obviously not sharing the same opinion. "Not really, sometimes it just works on its own, making people do things I didn't even want them to do. That is why I guess I should really be here then - so I can learn to control it. Not that I wish I had to be."

I couldn't help but laugh back. "Well, good luck with that. I have been here for weeks now and there is always some interruption or other when I'm training. I haven't even done a full session yet."

"What, really?" he replied, suddenly looking deflated.

I nodded. "Yup, sad to say. This place is useless so far." I pointed to Xavier and Hunter, "Those guys have been here for a year and are still no better."

"How comforting," he said, looking down as he played with the frayed thread on his jacket.

I clapped my hands together as I suddenly stood, trying to get away from the talk of all the negativity. "Well, anyway, want me to show you to the dorm rooms?"

Ben immediately jumped up as I finished and as I was showing him to his room, just as we entered through into the small courtyard space, he suddenly placed his hand on mine and looked down at me with the same creepy grin that was beginning to send an odd shiver down my spine. I didn't know if it was the way he dressed that made me feel strange—a very 1970s style cord pants and shirt with a vest—or his manner that disturbed me more. But since I had just met him, I held back the odd feeling for now and hoped that it would pass.

"Thank you, Lexia, I really appreciate it. I hope we get to know each other better while we are here," Ben smiled while holding my hand, shaking it for a moment too long. I forced back a fake smile to make it seem like I wasn't in a state of speculation, before forcibly removing my grasp from his and heading back into the common room. As I was walking back inside, Xavier casually leaned in the doorway as I passed.

"Whoa, someone wants to get into your pants," he said in his usual mocking tone. As I walked past him I let out a sigh, before quickly turning and mockingly slapping him over the head with my hand as I was beyond sick of his crude remarks.

"Hey, just stating the obvious!" he said, still smirking.

I ignored him, walked back inside, and folded my arms as I slumped back down on the sofa, giving a bemused look in reply as he sat beside me. I was about to shout some profanity over to him, as he kept smirking at me, but suddenly a voice blared into the room as the main doors swung open, sending a shock through me.

"Quick, Xavier and Lexia, we need your help! Come with me!"

And before we knew it, we were being dragged down the hall, once again having no clue what chaos we were about to enter.

Thirteen

After being dragged out of the dormitory, we were rushed down the halls, having no clue where we were going and going through endless checkpoints to get there. The guard eventually stopped us in front of a door that had grueling screams emitting from it. His hands trembling as he rattled the keys out of his pocket and aimed it for the lock.

"What is going on?" I urged to the guard, feeling uneasy as to whatever was happening, as he could barely hold the keys without nearly dropping them from his sweaty grasp.

His eyes shifted nervously as he eventually steadied his hands enough to unlock the bolt. "Well, Dana has sadly had another attack. Only this time, she is locked in the room with two staff members and if we don't get them out now, she could kill them."

Xavier narrowed his eyes and let out a grumbled sigh. "That is what you pay security for, don't you? I ain't doing someone else's job, especially when it doesn't benefit me in any way."

The guard turned his gaze to us, eyes gleaming as he pleaded. "Please, you two are the most powerful people in here right now as many of our guards had to be sent out to an incident. The reason we haven't asked the remaining guards is we don't want to hurt her and need this handled now. She is a big asset to our company."

"*Asset*?" I replied with confusion, as we were only here to reform. We didn't work here, which is the way he made it sound.

He suddenly looked shocked, as if the word meant something we shouldn't have known. "I don't mean *asset*, I mean we just want to help her as quick as we can, given you guys are the closest to us. I just need you two to go in there and use your powers to control her whilst I tie her down stab her with a shot. We will reward you if you complete this for us."

"Reward us how?" Xavier enquired through a raised brow.

The guard sighed. "We will come up with something, but we don't have time to talk about it now. Please can you do this?"

Xavier stared down at me, waiting for a response.

"Fine, but don't blame me if I blow up this place," I said, as he finally unlocked the door.

"Me neither," stated Xavier.

The guard gave a nod as we entered the room and the sight that greeted us wasn't for the faint of heart, that was for sure.

"You expect us to tame that crazy idiot?" Xavier said, scrunching up his face at the gory scene.

Blood was splattered all over the walls of the pale room as we gazed inside. There was nothing inside but the crazed side of Dana and the two seemingly lifeless bodies of the staff, who were both covered in torn red blotches from head to toe. Dana whipped her head around as we entered, cackling as she saw us.

"More snacks?" she beamed as our eyes met, no longer looking like the girl we knew anymore.

The guard stumbled back and clutched the side of the door. "Now, all you two have to do is keep her steady while I try and jab this into her neck, alright?"

"You know I can't control my power?" I muttered, for what felt like the hundredth time since I had arrived.

"Just please try Lexia or we'll have this cannibal on the loose and then we'll all be damned!"

I rolled my eyes and let out a deep breath. "Fine. Bloody hell. So, I guess I could distract her with a flame if I can conjure it up and you—" But before I could finish, Xavier walked over to the girl casually and suddenly pulled up the all too familiar beaming blue light from his hand.

"Good night," he smirked to Dana, as he sent a beam straight at her. She fell to the ground instantly, her whole body shaking as the electricity pulsed through her skin and lit up her veins with a vivid blue sheen.

"Xavier!" I shouted. "Why did you do that?"

He turned and shrugged his shoulders coolly. "Because you said yourself, you can't control your power. I can't be bothered to wait till you conjure it up. It's done now."

"Is she dead?" I asked as I stood behind him.

"Nope, just well and truly passed out," he said, as he turned back to the guard who was just standing there, like me, slightly dazed at the speed in which that just happened.

"There you go," Xavier smiled calmly to him.

"Uh... thanks..." The guard mumbled.

"We free to go?"

He nodded and gave us his key card so we could get through the gates and he could quickly get rid of us. We both left and headed back to the dorm; I was still shocked at how easily he had just done that.

"Thank you," I said to him. It was the first time I had been thankful to him at all and being kind to him left me feeling awkward.

A grin curled at his lip as he looked down at me. "Don't worry, I have your back. Plus, I don't want to die, just yet in case you did really blow up this place."

I couldn't help but laugh back. "Yeah, well, thanks anyway. Though, how do you have such control over your power?"

He shrugged his shoulders. "I don't. It was all chance really."

"What? So you just decided to chance it? Your brother said you do have control."

He nodded casually. "Pretty much. And he says a lot of things. In reality, I'm not that good, just slightly better than him. Don't tell him that though."

I couldn't help but laugh again. "You truly are crazy. I have no idea how you and your brother are related."

"Yes, I get that a lot. But, at least I got the cool genes. I mean, come on, teleportation?"

"Teleportation is better than what you can do!" I joked.

When I said those last words, he suddenly stopped and pinned me against the wall in the hall, both his arms blocking my escape as he put them on my shoulders.

"Oh really?" he smirked. "Why don't I show you another side of me—a side no one can match up to?"

My face blushed instantly; I had no idea why, as I couldn't stand the guy. But the redness couldn't help but blister at my cheeks as he stood inches away from my face. "There is no side I want to see of you, thank you very much," I said as I looked away.

"Hold back your judgements till first inspection. I'm not the type to let something go easily, until I've proven a person wrong."

I laughed. "Really? Then show me."

I suddenly caught him off guard with my remark, and he stood slightly back with widened eyes. "You serious?" he grinned.

"Of course, show me just how *good* you are?"

"No problems with that." He grinned and just as he leaned in for a kiss, I arched my leg and it went straight into the place that hurts.

"Ow, what the heck! Why do you keep hitting me?!" he shouted at me, flailing back in agony as he protected his manhood.

"You're a damn pervert, that's why I hit you! Just when I was trying to be nice to you, what do you do once again? You make me feel sick with hatred. Damn pig," I spat, before snatching the key card from him and storming down the hall as he fell to the ground, clutching his manhood in agony and shouting profanities at me.

As I walked ahead, I couldn't help but let a smile curl at my lip. I wasn't sure if I was happy this guy was getting to me or concerned but either way, I knew he was one to watch. Though in reality I knew I had bigger concerns to worry about, as what just happened back in that room seemed so odd. Why would they make us useless people tame her, when they have their own supernaturals who are way stronger and actually work at this place? They surely couldn't have sent out that many of their workers for them to have to use us. It was a strange situation indeed and one I knew was just making me wearier of this place.

Fourteen

Two weeks had passed since the arrival of our new roommate and let's just say, it had been an interesting two weeks at that. In those days since he had arrived, I had found out that my weird feeling about Ben was accurate, when he wouldn't seem to leave me alone. He seemed to have taken a liking to me and it wasn't going unnoticed. Every time he saw me, he would cling to me like a leech and no matter how many times I used profanities to tell him to stay away, he didn't absorb the words. I was stuck with him following my every movement. Colt had now turned to Ben.

My time here over the weeks so far had been very strange. I had hardly learned any way to control my powers and with all the chaos that was constantly happening, it was beginning to take its toll on me. I couldn't stand it here—nothing was getting done and I just wanted out. This was a trait of mine that had started after my father had passed. I had lived by his rules for so long that after he died, I felt freer and vowed never to let people control me again. This was why I became brash and often reacted over the top. I guess you could say I had a control complex, not just with my power but with things not going as fast as I wanted. However, as much as I hated the restrictions that were happening, I still knew I had to give this place a chance. More so, I had no choice as this really was my only option left if I wanted to live a normal life in the real world.

I sat at the breakfast table, dreading another day of failed training ahead. The sudden voice of Xavier entering the room made me let out a heavy exhale and as I could not be bothered to deal with his taunts so early in the morning, I fled into the common area and slouched onto the couch, where to no surprise, Ben joined me soon enough.

"You okay, Lexia? You are looking a little flustered today," he enquired in his usual soft tone as he sat next to me.

"I'm fine, Ben," I replied, while putting my hand to my temple to try and remove some of the building tension. "But could you please just leave me alone right now."

"Don't worry, Lexia, I don't think of you as a burden, I want to be here for you." He smiled, putting his hand on my leg.

I immediately narrowed my eyes his way. "Do that again Ben and you will be blown through that wall. Now, you either leave me be within five seconds or I will make you, your choice."

He immediately gulped, shuffled back and sat on the facing sofa, leaving me there to let out what must have been my fiftieth sigh that morning. My anger had been getting worse since I had arrived here. I thought I was going to get better being around people who understood and accepted one another. However, that was sadly far from the truth and these people were crazier than normal people. I was frustrated, tired, bored and wished I could just return to reality, no longer caring how horrid it had been. As I sat there withering away in my thoughts, Xavier came and sat on the sofas.

I felt his gaze on me immediately as he sat down facing me.

"Hey, Lexia," he muttered.

I knew he was trying to aggravate me because we never talked, other than to annoy each other. I closed my eyes and ignored his gaze, trying to set my mind on how I would proceed in this place, considering how slow everything was going.

However, as Ben's voice muttered my name in the background, I couldn't help but shoot my eyes back open.

"Is it true then, about why Lexia is here?" Ben muttered next to Xavier, but still managed to be heard by me.

Xavier smirked. "Very much so. She is truly crazier than anyone here."

"I thought so, her aura and everything radiates it," Ben replied, his bluntness taking me by surprise.

I slammed my hand down on the side of the sofa. "Do you mind not talking about me as if I was not in the room? It does nothing but aggravate me, which amounts to no good."

"Someone is touchy today," replied Xavier.

"Yes, I am, and if you continue talking to me, you will see more than just my touchy little attitude—now shut the hell up." Luckily, before my anger leaked out, we were called to start training. I sighed with relief as I could spend at least five minutes away from the pair.

I didn't know what was wrong with me, why I was suddenly more agitated by everything. I hated them, but I never cared enough to pay them that much attention, so I didn't understand why I was being so touchy. Though in reality, I knew it was because of the slow progress I was making. I was frustrated with the nothingness that was constant and how I still had no control because I rarely trained long enough. Even when I did stay for the full session, it made little difference.

However, there was nothing I could do but coast along, as in reality, I still somehow hoped it would all work out. That and the thought of turning out like my dad were the only reasons I fought on. However, I did now understand why he walked out from here—these people were seemingly useless! I just hoped that with the modern technology they had now, I would get somewhere and wouldn't have to run away like he did.

I soon proceeded with training, which involved me learning to steadily try and burn some paper while they timed how long I could hold the flame for before my nose started to bleed. Oh yes, nosebleeds were now a thing for me. Especially if I was using my power. I guessed the reason for this was because I was now using my power so often—every day—and it was straining my body to do this. It was annoying really, as it made my training sessions shorter because they didn't want to stress me out and make me bleed all over the floor. So every half hour I was given a break, allowing my body to calm down before I moved onto the next session.

As I sat on a couch in the waiting room for one of my nose bleed breaks, with my nose stuffed with paper towels, I overheard two voices whispering outside the frosted glass of the closed doors. It was a conversation that alarmed me and one that would begin to change the course of everything.

"Dr. Lincoln said the boy is ready to be injected with the solution soon. However, I'm not so sure. I'm still not certain his ability is worthy enough or that he could handle the amount of training at the unit, how about you?"

It was Miri's voice; the woman who often helped operate the training equipment and guided some of my training sessions. She kept her voice low as she muttered to someone beside her, whose shadow of a figure I could see through the frosted glass panels.

"I think he is ready. His control isn't the best and he is very fragile emotionally, but I think when his memory is erased, he will be a good strong asset to the team," replied a male voice I didn't recognise.

"Yes, I guess you're right. Anyhow, best get back to *training* these fools, eh?" Miri put an odd emphasis on the word 'training', which seemed to amuse them and they both laughed.

As they departed, I could feel nothing but a sense of confusion and intrigue. What they were talking about or more to the point, *who* were they talking about? But I knew, whatever it was, they were hiding things from us. From then on, I was aware there was more to this place than met the eyes and I was determined to find out what that was.

Fifteen

I didn't know what to do with the knowledge I had gained yesterday, as I truly wasn't sure what they had been talking about. However, the whole memory erasing part was what irked me the most. I had to tell someone about the odd knowledge I had now learned as I needed another opinion on the matter, in order to help at least try and ease my slow-growing suspicion of this place.

I decided to tell Hunter what had happened. However, no matter where I looked, I couldn't find him anywhere at all that day. Therefore, I had no other option but to turn to Xavier, who was sprawled on the couch, rifling through a catalogue of supernatural psychology magazines that we often used to study. Instead of reading them, he was just ripping out page after page, then setting them alight with electric blue flames, leaving a trail of black ash all over the marble flooring.

"You know, people do read those," I said as I headed his way.

"I told you, don't read this crap. It's useless." He smiled, continuing to light them up.

I rolled my eyes, as this was the least of my worries. "Whatever. Anyhow, have you got any idea where Hunter is? I can't find him anywhere."

He shrugged his shoulders casually and the usual annoying smirk—the one he seemed to reserve just for me—played at his lips. "Why, going to confess your undying love for him?"

I faked a laugh. "Hilarious. I'm serious though, any idea?"

He shrugged his shoulders again. "No idea think he is doing some extra training or something. Why do you need him?"

I let out a heavy sigh, just wanting to get this off my shoulders. "Nothing, I'll find him later."

Xavier suddenly stood up, brushing past the burned pages and oddly latching a hand around my wrist as I was about to turn away.

"Tell me. What's up?" he urged.

I turned back and looked at him. For the first time, there seemed to be a glint of concern in his eyes. This confused me more than anything. "No way, you won't take what I have to say seriously."

"I will, okay. I promise," he said, letting go of my wrist and placing his hand on his heart.

I narrowed my eyes but I so badly needed an opinion. "Fine, but one wrong word and forget it. Though, not here, somewhere in private."

I saw the glimmer arrive back in Xavier's eyes, but I caught him before he could shoot obscenities at me. "Don't!" I urged through gritted teeth.

He rolled his eyes. "Fine. Anyway, I have the perfect place to go. However, this, whatever you want to say, better be worth it because we could get in pretty huge trouble."

I nodded "Yes, it is. But since when did you care about getting in trouble?"

He laughed. "I don't, just thinking of you."

I rolled my eyes before he started dragging me toward the main door, pressing his hand up against the steel frame, which after a moment of hissing sounds, popped open.

"Let's go," he beamed. We rushed into the halls, running along and making sure no one was coming.

"What about the cameras?" I said, as I glanced passed the metal white boxes in the corners of the walls.

"Don't worry, I disabled them for now. How do you think I always manage to go about when I want. I use my electricity to play with them when I want by shooting bolts through their systems in the wall. It's great. I can switch them on and off whenever."

I give an understanding nod in response, before we eventually stopped at a fire exit and began climbing up the trillion steps. After the climb, he once again used his power to unlock another bolted door. As soon as it swung open, a gust of cold air brushed against my bare arms; something I hadn't felt in weeks, as the only outside air we were exposed to was in the small courtyard they let us use for a few minutes a day. Even then, you were guarded by four walls and just a small hole in the ceiling above, meaning that you didn't really benefit. It was amazingly refreshing to feel the beautiful gush hit past my skin again.

We walked outside to a cool dark view from the top of the building. We were much higher up than I had imagined. "We have this great place up here, but they only decide to let us out into a tiny courtyard for like, fifteen minutes a day? Are they serious?" I grunted, as we walked out further and I looked over the edge of the building, wrapping my arms around my body as the wind picked up. Although the view was still the dead stretch of space I remembered seeing upon arrival, somehow seeing it from up here at night and having the stars light up the sky from above, made it look like the ocean.

After a moment of appreciating the slight freedom and beauty of nature, Xavier spoke up.

"Now, what would you liked to discuss? It's almost dinner and I don't want to miss it."

I bit at my lip for a moment, not understanding why I felt so nervous about telling him what I had heard, but I needed to relay it to someone. Otherwise, I felt like I would explode. And even though he wasn't calming like Hunter, he had been here just as long, so I hoped he had some insight into what they could mean. "Well, it's about a conversation I overheard yesterday that kind of unnerved me."

"Everything here is weird so I'm not surprised," Xavier shrugged.

"Well, it's just that I overheard Miri and some other guy talking about removing someone's memory, as he was ready to be *free*, I guess. They said he was an 'asset'. I have no clue who they were talking about or even what they meant. However, how and why would they remove someone's memory? I don't understand."

Xavier's eyes drifted for a moment, seemingly pondering my words. I had no clue how to react either, but I was just glad I had at least told someone.

"Removing someone's memory, an asset?" he repeated, not seemingly as fazed as me now the words had sunk in. "This is a bit far-fetched. Maybe you just misheard?"

I narrowed my eyes. "I was literally a few inches away from them."

He shrugged his shoulders, which I couldn't help but be annoyed by. "I don't know what to say other than you are thinking too much into it. This is a government facility, there are going to be things happening that we don't know about."

I raised my brow. "And you are happy about that?"

"Hell no. But being here and living with secrets is better than me spending a stretch in jail. Not that they could hold me there, but that is beside the point. I live here for free and mostly do what I want."

"Well, that is good and all. But the way they were speaking, it was as if they were talking about one of us. What are your thoughts then? What if they meant you?"

Xavier turned and let out a sigh, placing his hands on my shoulders. "Lexia, they wouldn't have a chance with me even if they tried: I would wipe them out in two seconds. They could have been talking about anything, even an employee. We aren't the only supernaturals here, remember."

"So, you are telling me you trust these people?"

He laughed. "Of course I don't. I don't trust anyone. However, there is no point thinking over words when you have no clue what they were talking about."

I shifted his hands off my shoulders, as I was getting annoyed with his casual replies. If Hunter were here, he would have agreed with me or at least been more understanding. "Well, the way they talked made it seem like one of us. Just like what happened with Dana."

"What about Dana?"

"What, exactly! We don't know what has happened to her after you knocked her out. She could be one of their wiped-out zombies for all we know. And remember that guard saying she was an asset? That is the second time I have heard it now! I'm telling you, something is going on behind the scenes. Something with us we don't know about."

Xavier raised a brow. "Have you asked where she is?"

I shrugged my shoulders. "Well, no. But..."

"Exactly. So stop thinking into something when you haven't a clue. Just ask them. And I told you, there is going to be things happening we don't know about, but as long as it doesn't affect us, just ignore them."

I narrow my eyes. "Oh yeah, *just ask them*, that is a great idea."

"Well, do you want me to ask? I don't care?" he said as he started to walk back to the door.

"No!" I yelled. "You can't tell anyone this." I said, grabbing him by his sleeve. "Even if I am just thinking into something, I would rather keep what I heard secret."

He shrugged his shoulders. "Fine."

We stood there for another moment, just basking in the cold air. I guess he was right in a way—I had overheard the end of a conversation and they could have been talking about anything. Also, since I had been so frustrated with this place lately, maybe I was just internally mad at them and wanted to make a problem out of nothing. However, I still felt uneasy and from now on, I would keep a close ear out.

I suddenly felt Xavier's eyes look down at me and as I returned the gaze, his face gleamed in a way I had never seen before; like he cared.

"Don't worry, you know, because even if something did happen, I would always be there to help. That is why I am not as concerned as you," he said awkwardly, before suddenly taking a strand of my hair that was blowing in my face and tucking it behind my ear, holding his hand there for a moment too long. I just stood there confused and slightly shocked, as for the first time I was not hitting him back after he touched me.

It was odd. As we stood there and stared at each other, the calmest we had ever been, I felt comfortable. The moment only lasted a second though before Xavier pulled back, turning away and heading to the exit.

"You coming?" he smiled casually, digging his hands into his jean pockets.

I nodded and headed back to the exit.

"Thanks," I replied, as I walked down the stairs alongside him and for the first time, I actually meant the words. Even though we hadn't exactly agreed on things, I was just glad I had got the words out.

After that moment, I got to know Xavier a little more, and I couldn't help but feel a strange sense of comfort. It was so odd, as I went from pretty much hating the guy to thinking he was alright in such a short space of time and I couldn't help but wonder if I was losing the plot. I just hoped that it would keep up.

Sixteen

A week had passed since I had overheard the conversation in the training area and after I had talked with Xavier, I agreed that since I didn't really know the meaning behind their conversation, I would to put the subject to rest for now. Though I made sure to still keep my guard up, just in case.

I couldn't help but feel uneasy though, as I was such an honest person and having to fake myself around these people when I had such odd suspicions about them wasn't easy. However, I had no choice but to move forward and act like nothing was happening.

However, one morning as I was getting ready for training, my day turned into a whirlwind of chaos. After having had a conversation with Miri about my progress, they decided it was time to raise me up a few levels. And by a few, I mean far too many.

I would have been happy to be finally progressing, but when they told me they had shifted me straight from level 1 to level 7, I had a weird feeling something was happening that they didn't want to tell me. Given the little control I had and their previous experience with me, putting me on such a powerful level didn't seem right. I had hardly done any training over these weeks either, so it all just made no sense. They were playing a testing game and I didn't know yet as to why they wanted to keep playing me.

They guided me to the same room they had put me in for my first training session—the place I had almost blown up. I looked around the space and immediately felt uncomfortable as they quickly shut the door and locked me inside, leaving me feeling like a prisoner again. This did nothing but stress me out further.

"What am I doing back here?" I asked the staff, who were gazing at me through the window in the other room. I really hated coming into this room and had made them promise never to leave me in here anymore, so this did not help steady my nerves.

"We want you to practice conjuring up your power," Miri replied through the telecom, her expression way too calm for my liking.

"What? To what extent? Besides, I haven't even moved passed training level one correctly yet. I am so not ready. Therefore, I don't understand why you would test out level seven on me."

"We just want you to let your power through. You don't have to do anything crazy, we just want to see the strength of your ability. Still, more so than what you usually do. We want a larger scene."

I laughed, but their expressions remained stern. "You're joking, aren't you? You've seen what amount I can do anyhow, given the other trials. You know I can only light and somewhat control a *small* flame. I'm nowhere near the level of showing you more, haven't you learnt from past experience that this isn't right? And anyhow, you guys recently said I wasn't ready and wouldn't do this again until I was!"

"You have been doing very well lately, Lexia. As such, we think you are ready for this next big step now," Miri replied.

"You are kidding me, aren't you? No! I haven't done well and you want me to conjure up more of my power even though it could destroy this place? I can't, more so, I won't. I want to move up levels, but this is too dangerous and I don't want to pass out again." I started trembling a little, out of frustration now, as they didn't seem like they were going to budge.

"Lexia, you will be fine. Just don't think about anything while you are doing it. This will be a great exercise for you and will help you to be released sooner."

"I don't understand, why are we suddenly going so fast? I want to leave, but how is this going to help me if it hurts me. I have made zero progress over the weeks, so this makes no sense," I said, wondering how on earth they had come to the conclusion I was somehow doing well, when all they had done was complain about my lack thereof.

As I suddenly started to feel the pressure in the room drop, I knew what was about to commence. "We are starting to drop the pressure now in the room, all we want you to do is stop the force from dropping too low."

I began to feel the panic inside me kick in. "I can't do this!" I shouted. "Just let me out, I'm not ready for this level! I know I have been complaining about the length of the process and the fact I haven't learned much, but I can't do this! This is too much!"

However, they ignored my statement and continued to drop the pressure, averting themselves away from my gaze as the air was sucked out of the now unventilated space. It soon got harder and harder to bear and it felt like the air in my lungs was being suppressed. They knew what they were doing; when I got angry or stressed, my power tended to leak out uncontrollably. By dropping the air pressure in here, I would be forced to use my power to stop it from happening, by burning out the machines. They knew exactly what they were doing, I just didn't know why they were doing it this way.

"Let me freaking out of here!" I screamed, as I felt my breathing become heavier from the panic that was now setting in and the air tightening in the room.

"We can't, Lexia. You need to learn to control your power and since no other steps are working, we have to use this extreme way in order for you to move up," replied the other supervisor, whose brown eyes just stared at me coldly as he continued to remove the air.

"Please just stop, I can't handle this," I cried, tears beginning to stream down my face as I could no longer hold them back, knowing what was about to happen and how immense the pain would be not only physically, but emotionally. I knew that I would lose control again and that potentially, this would mean I would kill more people with my cursed power.

"This is how you first discovered your power: by going through a stressful situation when you were young. This may be the way for you to learn to control it, by going back to how it started and learning to control what stresses you first."

"This won't help!" I shouted. "This will only make things worse, just let me out. You said you wouldn't do this again till I was ready!"

Once again, they just brushed off my pleas. As I fell to the ground, clutching my neck for air, the memories of the explosion at college entered my mind. The fire, the screams, the death. I had blocked it all out until now and forgot about the fact I was a murderer. Even though I pretended not to care, inside my heart, I still did; that is why I hated this even more, as I didn't want to recall what had happened. The thought of being like my dad—something else I had tried to suppress—also came into my mind. My heartbeat picked up as the pressure continued to drop and as I glanced at my arms, my veins were starting to glow with the orange tinge that made me know trouble loomed.

"Stop!" I yelled again, as I clutched my head, trying to force down my power.

As that last word burst out of me, there was suddenly a commotion of voices coming from outside the door, but as the internal screams blared in and the pain and images of the past started to seep their way into the crevices of my brain, I found it harder and harder to latch onto reality and slowly, the cold dark room began to wrap itself around my mind. I gripped my hands to my head in agony to try and stop it all, trying so hard to suppress the fire from building up and bursting out. That was when I suddenly felt his hand touch me.

Xavier's cool palm latched itself around my arm, shaking my mind back into reality as he flung me into his arms and instantly flushed away the fire. My tears stained his shirt as his warmth suddenly poured around me and my mind returned to the scene around me.

"It's okay, Lexia. It's over now, I promise," Xavier whispered in my ear.

As I pulled away, his face was filled with calm. For that moment, I put my annoyances aside and couldn't help but instantly wrap my arms around him too. As my tears spilled down my cheeks, the pain started to mount in my head like it always did when my power tried to conjure itself up this fast and intensely.

After a moment of trying to regain my breath, flushing away past thoughts, and coping with the pain of trying to hold back my ability, I lifted up my head and gazed around the room to find I had once again just avoided a disaster: the walls were now riddled with deep fragmented cracks and singed edges. Alongside these were the dark glazed burn marks left by Xavier's electricity as he broke in. The observation window now had a huge dent in the middle and I sent a glare to the people who were still there, as they looked over to us in a flustered state.

"Let's get you out of here," he whispered and I gave a relieved nod in response. As we slowly got up and headed out the door, no one dared tried to stop us, especially not after the spectacle Xavier had just pulled.

"Won't you be in trouble for this?" I mumbled to him as he put me down and we stumbled out the room as I clung to his side for support. The staff now too frightened to utter a word after Xavier gave them a deathly glare.

"When did I care about getting into trouble?" he laughed, pulling me closer to his side as we trekked up the hall.

As we were heading back to the common room, the sound of a familiar pair of shoes began to click quickly behind us and Dr. Lincoln's voice suddenly chirped up in the background, ordering us to stop.

Xavier pushed me behind his back as he faced him and gave him a glare; I could feel the heat from his electricity warm up through my sleeve. "What do you want?" he spat, his eyes sparkling with fury.

"I'm sorry," Dr. Lincoln mumbled, looking rather dazed. "This was never meant to happen, I never should have gotten them to push you that far. I'm very sorry Lexia. Will you please forgive me?"

Xavier laughed. "Will she hell, you hurt her—again! Your promises seem to be riddled with crap."

Dr. Lincoln ignored Xavier's statement and kept his gaze on me. "Lexia, please understand. I was just trying to help. I thought you were ready, I was wrong. Please, stay and do not feel pressured, we will never make you do anything like this again."

"This isn't the first time though," I stated.

"I really am sorry, Lexia. You are so strong right now and I know you'll probably want to leave after that, but you can't, you have gotten so far."

"You expect her to stay after that? No way!" Xavier spat.

I bit at my lip, knowing I had little choice anyhow. "I have no choice, Xavier."

Xavier narrowed his eyes at me. "What are you talking about?"

"I have to stay here, I need the help."

Xavier tutted. "It's been weeks, they have done nothing for you. This place is useless—look at me for example. I have been here a year and Hunter is still a mess. Let's just get out of here. This place is obviously faulty and they are using us or something."

I shook free from his grip. "I can't, I have to stay."

Xavier stared down at me in disbelief. "After all that?"

I give a reluctant nod in response.

"She is right, I'm afraid. However, as you are staying, we will work on much lighter tasks from now on, I promise. This will never happen again." His smile didn't fill me with any reassurance, given this wasn't the first time I had heard these words.

"You promised that the first time around. I'm not ready to unleash my power to such a huge extent, okay? I will tell you when," I stated sternly, knowing that if they tried me again like that, I wouldn't hold back and would happily add them to my kill list.

Dr. Lincoln smiled. "I understand, Lexia. We will talk about this later as I have a meeting and I promise to work on getting better relations. I'm sure you want to rest after that."

We both gave nods in response, before I turned back to head to the common room.

"You are kidding, aren't you?" Xavier said as he followed behind me.

"Afraid not."

"But—"

"Xavier, let's just drop it now, okay. There is nothing I can do."

We walked back to the common room in silence, my suspicions having been verified that there was more to this place than met the eye. I was going to find out what was going on behind the scenes and why they were forcing my power out of me when they knew full well my progress was zero.

Seventeen

As I walked back into the dorm and Xavier grumpily disappeared into the kitchen, I headed back to my room as I could feel tears of frustration and exhaustion about to explode from me at any moment and it was not a sight I was used to people seeing. I was so tired of the slow progress in this place: I had been here for weeks and had little to no change in my control. I was now beginning to think all of this was a hoax because it wasn't just me; many of the others had been here ages and had made no progress whatsoever. I was beginning to trust my judgement of this place—that something about it wasn't right.

Just as the tears began to stain my cheeks, I bumped straight into Hunter, who was walking into the main dorm through the bedroom. And as I tried to brush past him to hide my ugly whimpering face, he grabbed me by the wrist and wouldn't let go until I turned to face him.

"Lexia, what's wrong?" he urged worriedly.

"I can't take this place anymore," I said, unable to hold back my anger, ripping my grasp away at the same time and heading into my room. Hunter closely followed and flipped me around at the shoulders to stare at him.

"Lexia, tell me what has happened?!" His eyes gleamed.

"Nothing, I'm just frustrated," I croaked.

"Guess they have done something to you again then?"

"What do you think?" I replied sarcastically, as I wiped away the tears.

"Want me to talk to them?"

I couldn't help but laugh. "What can you do?"

"Well, I can try and urge them not to be so harsh with your

treatment."

I shook my head. "Look, I'm fine, alright. Just having a moment of agitation take over. You can go now, honestly—I'll be fine."

"Look, I'm here if you ever need help. And so is Xavier, in his own weird way. I know he can be a pain in the behind, however, he really does care about you. He just shows it in a way that doesn't make it seem so."

"Nice to know," I joked and for some reason, I felt a sudden weird feeling towards Xavier tug at my heart. However, given what had just happened, I shook my head, as I didn't want to get more annoyed with his voice floating around my head.

"Thanks Hunter, you're a good friend."

"Glad you think so." He smiled.

"Anyway, I'm just going to rest a bit, okay? I'll be fine."

He gave a nod in response and smiled before we parted ways. For the next two hours, I couldn't shake off what he had said about Xavier. As even though it seemed like I was mad at him, deep in my heart, I was thankful for what he had done.

***

"Are you okay?" enquired Hunter as he entered the common room later that day. He had just finished training and I had returned from a failed sleep.

Before I could reply, Xavier entered the vicinity too, after having hidden in his room for most of the day like me. "No, she's not," he replied bluntly, as he slumped down on the sofa and looked at me through a narrowed gaze.

I rolled my eyes. "I can't help this, Xavier. You think I want to stay in this damn place? I can assure you, I do not. But, here is better than the life of rubbish that awaits me out there—a life without control of this thing that is killing me."

Xavier just folded his arms and tutted. Hunter just stared between us with widened eyes, confused as to what was going on "What exactly happened?"

"Well, Lexia nearly blew up the place again when they forced her to bring up too much of her power, yet she wants to stay here," Xavier interjected.

"Where am I supposed to go? They would only drag me back here anyway!" I shouted.

Xavier gripped the side of the sofa. "I would go with you, I told you. I would protect you!"

"Why would I want to be with you, I can't stand you?!" I urged.

"Well, it's better than being here after that, I assure you."

"Well, leave then, if you want to."

Xavier smirked. "Why would I do that? I enjoy annoying you."

I give him a glare back.

"I'm so confused right now," said Hunter scratching his head.

The conversation was soon diverted when I was called to see Dr. Lincoln and as I was escorted to a small office not far from the training area, I walked into the room and was greeted by more people than just him. All their cool gazes bore into me, as I was instructed to sit down at a large table in front of the five other people that surrounded Dr. Lincoln, who was sitting in the middle of them looking rather uneasy.

"Hello Lexia. Two meetings in one day, you must be sick of the sight of me," said Dr. Lincoln, trying to break the odd tension in the room. However, when I didn't reply, the awkwardness continued to grow. He cleared his throat as he continued, "Anyhow, we have something very important we would like to discuss with you. Something that may confuse you, but all we want you to do is hear us out, okay?"

I shrugged my shoulders in response. "What is it?" I grumbled, as I didn't want to be here right now; I was still raging inside, which was evident by the fact my veins contained an orange hue. That said, I could feel something interesting was coming and I had to stay to find out what.

One of the other glum looking people sitting next to Dr. Lincoln suddenly slid over a piece of paper to me. All that was written on the front was the word *Lucida* in bold black lettering.

"What is this for?" I said, shaking the paper in the air.

"I know this is a lot to ask," urged Dr. Lincoln, "especially given what has happened today. Also, I'm kind of back tracking on the words I said to you earlier, but I would love it if you could show everybody just a small amount of your power."

I immediately sent a glare his way. "You are kidding me, right?" Then just as I proceeded to get up out of my chair to leave, as I couldn't deal with any more of these lies today, a hand wrapped itself around my shoulder, forcing me to sit back down. "What the hell?" I yelled, as the guard stood firmly by my side.

"It's very important that you do this, Lexia. These people are here to evaluate you, to see your power," Lincoln said, pushing his glasses back to his eyes.

"Evaluate? We have already done that, weeks ago. You have seen what I can do?"

Dr. Lincoln laughed. "Yes, I know that. However, these people have not and they would like to see you perform a little, it's very important."

"So, all you want me to do is burn this paper, then I can go?" I said through narrowed eyes, as I couldn't be bothered with any more drama.

He gave a nod in response.

"Fine," I said under my breath, while placing my hand over the piece of paper and channelling as little energy as I could, but enough to burn the edges of the paper without igniting anything else.

"That enough?" I said, adding a hint of sarcasm to my tone.

"Perfect," replied the person who had handed over the paper, as he took back its burnt fragments and examined it as if it was some ancient specimen. For a moment, they talked amongst themselves, nodding and chatting about things I couldn't make out, before their gazes directed back to me and the uneasiness in me seemed to grow even more.

"Lexia, we have a proposition to offer you," Dr. Lincoln said suddenly. "We would like to offer you a job here at Lucida as one of our protection officers. We think you have tremendous potential and would be a great asset for the company."

I almost wanted to laugh at what he had just said. Were they seriously trying to recruit me as part of their team—a delinquent misfit who was here to be transformed into a model citizen?

"You are kidding me, right?" I said, a smile curling at my lip in amusement as I finally realised they hadn't been training me—they'd been testing me to see if I was worthy of one of their jobs.

All their faces remained cold as they looked at me. "We are very serious, Lexia. We would love to have you as a part of our government team. There will be great rewards for you, if you join."

I narrowed my eyes. "Wait, is this why you have been testing me, to examine me more than train? Is that why I have not been gaining any progress at all. This was all purposeful." Apart from the moments chaos kept erupting during the sessions, there had been plenty of times that I should have learned something, when all was quiet. But there had been nothing and now I understood why.

Dr. Lincoln laughed. "Somewhat. We were originally going to train you here. However, we saw how special your ability was and the potential it had but training it up here would mean nothing since it is so powerful. So, we did decide to just watch and test you instead by seeing how strong your power was. I'm sorry about this but we had to do it this way in order to make sure you could be a good candidate to work for us. Lexia, wouldn't you like to hear about the rewards?"

"Not really," I stated plainly, as the offer did little to interest me, given that I hated the fact they had been testing me without my knowledge and not training me at all. I had wasted all of this time.

"Whatever you like, you can get. A new life, gifts, whatever. They are yours. If, you agree to work for the company and train in our special unit."

"Special unit?"

"Yes, there is a place with even better training technology you would use. This is where the true training takes place, meaning faster treatment to learn to control your powers."

"Wait, faster control? Why don't you use the technology here then?"

"Because, we only have so many of these top quality machines and sadly, we have to reserve them for the best. And we think you are just that."

I nodded in response, but it still felt as if something was off. Faster control. It sounded amazing, but in reality, I still couldn't trust these people enough to believe what they were saying when they had fooled me into thinking they were training me. However, I still continued, sounding as if I was interested. More so, I was just curious.

"I suppose faster control does sound nice and I guess I understand you have to keep some machines for special cases. But, why do you want me? I'm useless."

Dr. Lincoln laughed. "You aren't useless. I know it seems like we have lied to you, but we have just been observing your abilities so we can decide if you are the right fit for the true training program."

"True training program? So, what have I been doing then, wasting time?"

"You have been training to some degree, but just not with our best equipment. Anyhow, Lexia, this is a golden opportunity. One that your father never had. Don't you want to be able to make yourself into something and not compare yourself to him all the time?"

As soon as he said those last words, it all sounded more appealing. "I don't want to become him. Would I still live here though?"

He nodded. "Of course, just in a different part of the building. However, this job isn't for the faint of heart. There is an immense amount of training that goes into it."

"Hey, slow down—just because I am enquiring doesn't mean I want to work for you. You think I can trust you, after you have tested me the way you have?" I shot back.

Dr. Lincoln rested his hands on the desk. "This is a great opportunity for you, as you will be living with other like-minded supernaturals. You would never have to feel like an outsider again. And they all have control so they will be a great influence."

The last thing I would ever want to do is work for the government, but at the same time, the prospect of having my own life did sound tempting, as did not turning out like my father.

"What exactly would this job entail?" I enquired.

"You would be protecting the company for us and dealing with any matters we required—nothing too crazy. Just think supernatural protection. You will have to live here. However, you can have whatever you desire and make this place your own."

Dr. Lincoln sure had a way with words, but as these people looked at me the conversation I had overheard the other day popped into my head and made me feel uneasy. I could still tell what he was saying wasn't completely true and normally, I would have said something, but these people gave off bad vibes. Until I knew the full reason as to why I felt so uneasy, I wasn't going to say anything nor agree.

I decided to play it the safe way. "This does sound interesting, but do I have to make up my mind now?"

Dr. Lincoln smiled. "Of course not, we can give you some time if you like. This is a great opportunity and not many people receive it, so the more you think about it, the better."

"Thanks, I will definitely think hard about it." I was definitely going to think about it alright. And discuss it with Hunter and Xavier because I needed a second opinion.

I had to find out the reason why I felt so uneasy about this place, besides the lies, and this was the perfect opportunity to do so. Because at the end of the day, why would they want to recruit someone as dangerous and destructive as me? But, then again, that may just be the reason.

Eighteen

Two days had passed since I was invited to join the company and in those two days, I hadn't seen Hunter nor Xavier, which was really annoying and stressful. I needed to talk to them about what had happened, but they seemed to have just disappeared. That was until I came back to the dorm after another failed training session that they were still making me go to and they were both sat on the sofas looking rather glum. They didn't even look up at me as I entered the room and as I walked closer, I saw they both seemed to be in deep thought.

"Are you guys okay?" I asked them, which seemed to send them into a momentary state of shock as their eyes suddenly darted up at me.

"Oh, yeah. Just thinking, you know..." Hunter said, trailing off.

I sat down next to him on the couch and stared at his blanched face, his calm nature radiating with an odd amount of angst which I had never felt from him before. "Where have you guys been? I have some news I need to relay."

Hunter cleared his throat, seemingly dazed, "Oh, you know just…"

Xavier suddenly butted in before he could finish, "None of your concern, that is where—now just leave, will you. We are in no mood to hear your rubbish."

"Bloody hell, you still mad about the other day? Forget it already!" I yelled.

Xavier gave off an odd laugh. "I couldn't care less about that. We have our own problems, okay? We don't need to have yours too."

"Xavier, calm down," Hunter pleaded.

Xavier shrugged his shoulders. "Well, she keeps coming to us with her problems, we don't need them."

"Thought you said you would protect me?" I urged jokingly.

"Why? Do you need protecting? Doesn't seem so. Now leave, Lexi."

"Bloody hell! What is your problem?!" I said.

"Guys, calm down, alright!" Hunter said, looking annoyed. "Look, Lexia, we just got some news which wasn't too good, okay. That's why Xavier is angry. So, we were locked away for two days and I stayed by his side to calm him down. He's just annoyed. It's best to just leave him when he is like this."

"Why, what happened?" I urged.

Xavier darted his eyes towards Hunter, seemingly urging him not to tell me, but he did so anyway. "Well, we got told we will have to be here even longer than we thought. He thought our release date was going to be soon. I knew it wouldn't be since I still haven't got control over my power, and this is all my fault."

"For God's sake Hunter, I've told you this is because of me and my damn anger. This isn't your fault!"

In that moment, I saw just what it was like to care for a sibling. Even though they hardly seemed to speak in reality, I sensed that they were super close and for that, Xavier went up in my estimations a little. Hunter just looked to the ground, however, not his usual chirpy self and seeing him like this almost broke my heart, since I did consider him as a friend. I knew right now wasn't the time to share my news, as they needed to process their own problem. As such, I decided to let them somewhat grieve in peace, as I knew how annoying it was when you just wanted to be left alone.

I let out a soft sigh as I jumped up from the couch. "I see. Well, I'll leave you guys to your minds. See you later."

They didn't stop me and instead seemed to welcome it. I headed into the kitchen to wallow over my thoughts, slumping down at the kitchen table, as one thousand questions raced through my mind.

Why weren't they training us properly in this part of the facility? Surely they wouldn't recruit everyone and therefore the others still needed to be trained so they could eventually leave? How had Elisa been trained so fast and left so early, had they offered her a job too and never told us? Why had they been here so long? Why was I so uneasy about this whole place? Why was I so convinced that they were hiding even more lies?

I needed answers and I needed to ask someone that had been here longer than me, to hopefully get some insight about this place and to figure out why they would offer me a job. Useless old murderous me.

As Colt suddenly walked into the kitchen and our eyes met, his widened a little and immediately went to turn around and head back out the door, something he had been doing every time I was in the vicinity.

"Hey Colt," I said, deciding to ask him if he knew anything about what this company did, besides *train* us like idiots.

He stopped in his tracks and gulped. "Yeah, Lexia...?"

"Can you come here a minute, I want to ask you something."

After a moment he reluctantly came over and sat in the seat beside me, which I had to usher him to do. "Hey, haven't talked in a while, how you been? Putting any more accidental curses on people?" I joked.

Colt's eyes widened even more as I said the words, which made me instantly regret them. I had already forgotten about the incident so I didn't even understand why he was still so scared of me. Yet, I did threaten him and given that I had killed people, I guess I understood. "I'm only joking Colt, I actually want to ask you something."

He seemed to relax a bit after that, but it did bug me he wasn't his usual annoying self around me and hadn't been since the incident.

"What do you know about Lucida?" I said, forcing a smile.

Colt bit at his lip for a moment, seemingly pondering over my question and surprised it wasn't something worse. He let out a soft breath before he replied, "Well, what type of thing do you want to know?"

"Well, I know why I'm here and stuff, obviously, but do you know more about what goes on, behind the scenes?"

"Well, I guess they just monitor our progress and stuff. I'm not sure. Apparently they also work closely with the government in other means too."

"Like what?"

"I don't know if it's true, but I've heard they try and recruit certain supernaturals and make them work for them. I doubt it's true though because I'm sure they would have recruited Elisa. I mean, I doubt they would let her go with the ability she had—she could have created a whole dead army for them if she had wanted to."

His words caught me off guard and I felt slightly out of comfort at the fact he had said out loud what I had thought and realised it had been stupid to ask him about this when I was keeping it on the down low. But I never expected him to say something like this. I soon ended the conversation remembering cameras lay everywhere. So, it was true. They had recruited others, maybe even Elisa for all I knew, and I needed to find out who they had. I had seen Elisa's power and although she did have decent enough control, it still did not warrant the fact she had been let go so early. I was now truly beginning to think they had offered her a job too and that this part of the facility was just like a zoo. Like they were watching us to see our powers in person, testing them and then trying to recruit the people they saw with the most potential. That was all that made sense in my mind.

As I was locked up in here, I doubted I could find out these other supernaturals to see if my theory was true. However, they did say they lived here, so maybe if I did agree to go, I would have a chance to meet them and investigate more. I would have to see, but I needed to know more about this company first before I even dared think of what lay beyond.

Nineteen

A few days had passed since not only my job offer—which I still hadn't made up my mind about yet—but also the conversation between Hunter and Xavier.

They had calmed down a little. However, they had pretty much kept to themselves over the past few days and I still hadn't told either of them what was going on. I needed to though, and soon, because I could tell the people who had offered me the job were getting increasingly anxious each time I told them to give me some more time. This confused me as I didn't understand why they needed to hurry me so much. But still, I needed to make up my mind and soon. However, I needed their opinions because they had been here so long and knew pretty much the workings of this place. Xavier, in particular.

As I walked back into the common room after having had another conversation with Dr. Lincoln about postponing my answer, I saw Hunter sitting silently on the couch, the fire roaring by his side as he looked intently into his *Teleportation for Dummies* book. He had not been himself since the other day and it actually made me feel upset for seeing him this way. Even Xavier not being his usual obnoxious self was starting to make me feel uneasy. I couldn't believe I was thinking it, but I oddly missed his crude ways.

Letting out a sigh, I sat on the couch facing Hunter, who didn't even acknowledge I was there, which was so unlike him. I tapped my fingers against the velvet of the sofa, trying to conjure up words to start out with, but for some reason as I saw him there so immersed in his world, with his own problems, I just couldn't bring myself to talk to him about anything.

Normally he would be the first one I wanted to talk to, but he was so lost in his own thoughts that I still couldn't utter my problems. So, even though I didn't want to, I decided Xavier was probably the best one to talk to about this, as he tended to still give straight answers.

"Do you know where Xavier is?" I asked Hunter.

He shrugged his shoulders casually, not removing his eyes from his book. "I'm not sure, I think he is somewhere in the facility."

Thanks a lot, I thought to myself. However, I did know of one place he might be—the place he took me to the last time, where he often went when he had a lot on his mind.

I gave a smile to Hunter, who still ignored me, before I headed to the door, wondering how on earth I was going to unlock the thing. I had never done small controlled tasks before—only major explosions, like at my college. I certainly had never tried to unlock a door.

However, I tried anyway and placed my hand near the door's lock like Xavier had. Then I let my power try and do the work. I imagined the lock unbolting, melting slightly and then the clicking of each mechanism becoming unhinged. Before I knew it, that's what happened. I heard the door click open and as I pressed down on the handle, the door swung out. I let out a smile, impressed that I had actually done it and managed not to burn down the place in the process.

I turned to look in the room to make sure no one was looking and as Hunter kept his head firmly pressed in the book, seemingly uninterested, I ran out into the hall and headed to Xavier's secret space on the roof.

I quietly trailed through the corridors, remembering to short circuit the security cameras like Xavier had. I opened the door to the fire exit, climbed the mound of stairs, swung open the door to the roof, and as the cool breeze brushed by me, I saw Xavier leaning casually against the edge of the building, looking down onto the stretch of emptiness that lay ahead.

I let the door swing shut as I knew he wouldn't want to talk to me, but I had to get his opinion and he was the only person I could ask. As I headed over and stood next to him, leaning against the balcony wall to look out at the view, he seemed to have broken out of a daze as our eyes met and he stumbled back a little in shock.

"Bloody hell, Lexia. What are you doing here?" he said with widened eyes.

"Just came to see how you were," I smiled.

He narrowed his eyes and leaned his arms back against the wall, looking out at the view. "Well, thanks. But I don't need to be checked on."

I shrugged my shoulders. "I don't mind. You've been quiet. I just decided to see if you were okay."

He turned his head slightly towards me, not believing a word of what I was saying. "So, you haven't just come up here to lumber me with all your problems then?"

I scratched my head and laughed. "Well, that was my second part, but I really did come to see if you're okay."

"Well, I'm just dandy, Lexi. Now, sorry but like I said the other day, I have my own problems to deal with right now, so if you don't mind…"

"They offered me a job—" I spouted, no longer able to hold back the words that were mentally crushing my brain.

Xavier just stood there for a moment with a raised brow, trying to comprehend my words. "What are you talking about?"

I cleared my throat. "Dr. Lincoln and some other people offered me a job, to work and live here as their sort of 'apprentice' supernatural."

Xavier narrowed his eyes even further, gritting his teeth in the process. "They offered you a job doing what?"

I shrugged my shoulders. "They didn't give me the full details, they just said they would like me to be one of the company's protectors and to do some odd jobs for them."

"Did you accept?"

I shook my head. "Not yet, but that is why I needed to talk to you. I want to know your opinion on the company since you have been here a while. Do you think I should take it?"

Xavier pursed his lips for a moment. "It's like any other government supported facility—corrupt and confined. Their way or no way."

"So, do you think I should take it?" I urged after an eye roll.

Xavier turned his body to me. "You want to work for something so corrupt and confined?"

I shrugged. "They said they would pay me and I would work with other supernaturals."

"And you can't get paid in the real world?"

I let out a sigh. "The difference is I would be accepted here, not in the real world."

Xavier shook his head. "In all seriousness, I wouldn't work here. Do your time, then get out. Working for the government is never a good thing, I know that for a fact after having lived here and watched them for so long. Besides, didn't you say you hated this place?"

"I do, but—"

"But nothing. My advice, leave while you can." He narrowed his eyes. "What I don't understand though, is why they would offer you a job when you have no control over your power and have shown no progress these last few weeks, when I have been here for a while and *have* control."

He did have a point and it was one of the reasons I was confused too, as I saw myself as being useless with my abilities. And although they said they would train me more with this amazing new equipment, given the way things were going at the moment, what else could they do anyway? However, when it came to Xavier not being recruited, I realised what his problem was and shrugged again. "Maybe your anger is the problem?"

"Guess, you're right," Xavier said and we both couldn't help but laugh.

Even though this conversation hadn't quite gone the way I wanted, I knew talking to him would be better now I had gotten to know him more because he was so blunt about things. He was right, I had said I hated this place and so taking a job here wouldn't be a great idea, no matter how much they paid me. Besides, it wouldn't be like I could spend it anyway.

"You do have a point, I must admit. After those things I overheard a while back, I don't even know why I am considering this. Maybe just so I didn't have to go back to my old life since they said I would live here as well, but in reality, it is better than being stuck in this place, which makes me feel so on edge. I guess I wanted to do it so that I could know more about all of this."

Xavier nodded. "I am curious about it too. However, I am still confused why they asked you when your power is useless," he joked.

"Hey, at least I can control my anger!" I laughed back, though in reality it was a lie.

And for that moment, as we kept shooting back jokes to each other, I saw Xavier's true smile for the first time and couldn't help but see the real him. It was so good to see him peppy again, smirking or otherwise. It confused me as to why I felt so happy to see him like this because our relationship was so fickle, but in reality, I loved seeing this side of him back. After a few moments of silence as we gazed out over the nightscape, we suddenly turned our heads to face each other and as our eyes met and the stars shone above us, it was like something sparked in that moment as we stood there so vulnerable. It was like a light switch flicking on; we were the only two in the space around us.

"I have a question," he suddenly said, breaking the moment.

"What is it?"

"Do you like my brother?"

I oddly felt like blushing as he said the words, even though I had no reason to, as I only thought of Hunter as a friend.

"No, not romantically anyway, if that's what you mean. Why are you asking that?"

"Are you sure?"

"Yes, I'm sure. He is just a cool friend—more like a brother to me if anything. Now, why are you asking this?"

"Because, I just wanted to know before I do this," he smiled, before he leaned in for a kiss and threw everything between us off balance.

He put his hand up and caressed my cheek, leaning forward. As our lips met for the first time, it was like the tension between us in that moment broke and faded into the dark abyss that surrounded us. And though it was only a momentary blip as we soon pulled back, both our cheeks burned with redness, as I don't think we ever expected this to happen.

Xavier turns back to face the view, trying not to show his cute embarrassment. "Sorry, I uh…"

I couldn't help but feel awkward, but at the same time, I couldn't hold back a laugh as I saw this new cute and slightly innocent side to him. And realised he was suddenly apologising for it.

He looked at me, confused as to why I was laughing. "What's so funny?" he mumbled, clearing his throat shyly.

"Nothing, I just didn't expect it, that's all. And your face is so cute."

He couldn't hold back his laugh. "Hey, don't call me cute!"

"Just stating what I see." I smiled while leaning against the railing.

I didn't know how to feel about what had just happened and what would happen afterwards. However, I knew that seeing him smile like this had started to chip away the fragments of negativity about him I had in my heart. I just wondered how long this moment would last before we bickered again.

Twenty

Almost overnight, Xavier and I went from basically hating each other, to pretty much being a cute awkward couple. Yet, we had obviously not declared that fact as I still felt like it was all way too much, too fast. In fact, I couldn't help but feel strange around him and I knew he felt the same. He still kept up his arrogant act—it just wasn't as harsh. I think Hunter seemed to have sensed something too, but it didn't seem like Xavier had told him about our kiss.

I knew Hunter wouldn't say anything though because he had been acting so differently; it was like his whole personality had been drained from him and it was heartbreaking to see. I knew he felt like he was dragging his brother down because his training was getting nowhere, but this much darkness surrounding him was ridiculous and I just hoped he would snap out of it soon.

The day after our awkward kiss, I woke up and bumped straight into Xavier and his shirtless body in the dorm hall. He stared down at me with a smile, his curled dark locks still damp from the shower. It oddly made me blush to see him like this and then all of a sudden, his lip curled up into his usual devilish smirk. He suddenly dragged me inside his room, locking the door. He pushed me up against the door and put his hands either side of me; I was now unable to hold back my ever-reddening cheeks.

"What are you doing?" I muttered, trying not to show my nerves.

Xavier's expression lingered with his typical mischievous attitude. "Nothing, just gazing at you," he simply stated, moving closer and closer until I could feel his breath against the skin of my neck. I could feel my face beam brighter each time he inched his face towards mine, until I couldn't hold back a nervous laugh anymore. He looked so cute with his freshly-washed damp brunette curls that flowed softly against his forehead.

As I gazed down at his naked torso, my cheeks getting even redder in the process, I couldn't help but notice the masses of burn marks on his chest and as he watched my eyes trail down to the deep red, healed-over slits, he soon shuffled away and put a shirt on.

"Sorry, didn't mean to stare," I said, wanting to kick myself.

We soon went and sat on the edge of his bed as he threw a t-shirt over his torso, covering up the red dents. His face simmering down in the process. "Want to know how I got them?"

I shrugged. "You don't have to tell me, if you don't want to,"

"It's fine. I just used to take the punishments for my brother when we were younger, as he was never really good in school and so, our parents used to hit me with a boiled stick. That's what the scars are."

My eyes widened. "They used to what? Just because he wasn't good at school?"

He nodded. "Sadly yeah, that is why we ran away two years ago—couldn't take any of their rubbish anymore. That is why Hunter gets so emotional and depressed, because he feels guilty about what I went through. I tell him I'm his brother, so of course I'm going to stick up for him, but he just can't help but feel guilty."

I was stunned at how honest he was suddenly being towards me. "Wow, you are such a good brother. Maybe you are not such an arrogant fool after all," I replied, now understanding why Hunter was still so down, as the guilt of them being here so long must have been eating away at him. He must have felt useless.

"Well, I try to be a good brother. Though I have put him through hell with all my rebellion and all, so I guess you could say we are even."

"Did your parents know about your powers?" I enquired.

He shook his head. "Of course not. That would have just given them another reason to beat me. They were highly religious, so you do the math," he said, shrugging and leaning back casually on the bed. "Anyway, I have something to ask you too," he stated out of the blue. "Did you really blow up your college?"

My eyes widened a little at his question as it was still so early to be talking about such dark moments in our lives. However, since he had opened up, I let out a sigh and nodded. "Sadly, it's true."

"How come?"

"Well, in short terms, I had held my power in for so long that it exploded from me at college. No control plus holding down an ability that craves a release is not fun to have to deal with. Basically, I did not want to let it out, but my aunt was sick of me hiding away from my problems. The stress of everything just hit me in that moment, especially as bullies were taunting me. That was the final thing that made me go *boom*—it got its release."

"I see. So, did they blame you?"

"Of course not. They just suspected it was an accident, even though they couldn't find a cause. They are never going to think something supernatural, thankfully."

"Did anyone get hurt?"

I gulped at that question, as I wondered whether he could bear the response that I had killed people. I was surprised at the same time he didn't know this. But it must not have been something he had read on my report. Then I remembered he had tried to kill the police, so if he didn't respond well, then he wasn't exactly innocent either. "Yeah, people died. It wasn't fully my fault though. It was just the bullies that died, as they were the only ones closest to me at the time. Everyone else managed to escape. They should have left me alone, then none of this mess would have even happened. Not in that building anyway. This is just what my aunt told me, so I don't know the full truth really."

"Wow, that's crazy. Though, how do you feel about it all, their deaths?"

"Does it sound morbid to say, I care but don't at the same time?" I asked.

Xavier shrugged. "Not to me. They shouldn't have tested you."

"But, I suppose they didn't deserve to die, did they? They didn't know I had this ability."

"I suppose not. However, this wasn't your fault anyhow. You can't control that flame thrower inside of you. It's not like you wanted it to happen." Xavier suddenly put his arm around my waist and lay me down next to him. "Anyhow, it won't ever happen again. I'll protect you."

As I turned my head and our eyes met, our lips met once again, but this time I made it stop, as his words rang through my head. "Don't say things like that."

"What?"

"You'll protect me and stuff. I don't like it."

"How come?" he said.

"I can protect myself."

"Okay, Miss Superior. Damn, sorry for caring."

I rolled my eyes. "It's not that, I just want to do things on my own."

I don't know what suddenly came over me, but this all suddenly felt too much. I was here to learn to control this monster inside of me once and for all, not play around with a guy that annoyed the hell out of me, so I didn't even know what I was doing. I sat up and let out a sigh, knowing this was neither the place nor time for this. Especially not when I needed to watch the place.

"What's wrong?" Xavier enquired at my sudden change of attitude.

"Nothing, it's just… I can't be doing this right now."

"What?" said Xavier, sitting up next to me.

"*This*. Romance and stuff. I need to focus on myself, I'm sorry."

Xavier laughed. "*This*. Look, if you don't like me, just say. Don't waste any more of my time chasing after you."

I tilted my head. "That isn't it. I just need to focus on learning to control my powers and watching these liars that run this place, not the next time I'm going to kiss you." I bit my tongue as I said the last part. I felt my cheeks beaming as I saw Xavier's mischievous smile return.

"So, you have been thinking about it then?" he joked.

I rolled my eyes and got up. "Whatever. Look, I have to go and get dressed now alright, but please heed my point."

"Oh, I will. However, don't expect me to stop myself when I see you in those cute shorts of yours," he joked and I couldn't help but roll my eyes as I left the room.

I was serious about this though and I knew it was going to be hard to stay away from him. Not just because we lived so close together, but because I generally did have an odd liking for him and that was the problem. I needed to focus on myself, but at the same time, I knew that was probably going to be impossible.

Twenty-One

Over the next few days, I tried my hardest to keep away from Xavier. However, he sure was persistent and tried his best to stay constantly by my side. I'd had enough one day and needed to calm down, so I stayed back while the others went to training. However, as I entered the common room, I saw Hunter staring at his *Teleportation 101* book, with the same sullen face he'd had for what felt like eternity.

I sat in front of him as he flipped through the pages, not even noticing I was there until I cleared my throat and muttered a *hello*. To which, he just gave a nod in response. I couldn't take this version of him anymore though, I needed the old Hunter back so we could talk and laugh about things.

"Hunter, can I ask you something?" I said.

He didn't even look up from his book and muttered, "If you must."

"Why are you acting like such an idiot?"

He looked up and closed his book, seemingly shocked by my choice of words. "I'm not."

I laughed. "Well, obviously you are. You have barely spoken two words to anyone, even your own brother."

Hunter let out a sigh and I could tell he was trying to hold back his emotions "I have nothing to say, Lexia."

"You have nothing to say? That's a first," I joked.

"Look, I just can't be bothered with this right now, can you give it a rest?" He was just about to get up and leave, but I did so as well and grabbed his shirt sleeve.

"Look, just talk to me, let out whatever is bothering you. I'm here for you just like you were for me." I knew it was about his brother, but still I wanted to hear it in his own words before I pre-judged the situation.

Tears started to well up in his eyes and I knew he was trying his hardest not to crumble. I zoned around the room to make sure no one was about. "Come with me," I stated, latching onto his hand and dragging him into my room.

"Lexia, I—"

"Just sit down," I interrupted, as I shut the door behind us. He did so straight away, trying to wipe away his tears before I could see them as I sat down next to him.

"You were the first one to be there for me when I came here and so I want to do the same for you. Please just let me know what is going on, you really have me worried."

For a moment he just sat and stared at the ground, but I could tell he couldn't hold it back any longer and the tears started to flow.

"I'm just sick of all of this," he sighed. "Sick of hurting everybody."

"Hurting everybody? Who are you hurting?"

"My brother, my family, everyone!" he blurted back.

I knew about his family and what they had done, but I didn't dare relay that as it could dishearten him. "Is this about you and your brother? Look, he really cares about you."

"I know, but what use am I? I was terrible at school, at my power, and now at this place. I've been here for a year. He learned to control his power ages ago and I'm still here, being useless and stopping him from moving forward, once again."

It broke my heart to see him like this. "You can't think like this. He is here to support you and that is why he sticks around. If he truly felt you were letting him down he wouldn't have stayed, would he."

I passed him a tissue and he wiped at his tear-stained cheeks. "I guess you are right. I just can't help but feel like this, you know. It's all finally got on top of me. Sorry for being so cold, I just didn't want to burden anyone else with my presence."

"We're friends, aren't we? That's why I'm here for you—to listen." I smiled.

"Well, you sure are one good friend. How have you been anyway?" he enquired through a sniffle.

"The usual, you know, just trying to learn to control my pain-in-the-butt abilities too." I laughed.

"Yeah, I sure know what you mean."

After that we just sat and talked and I couldn't explain how nice it was to see this raw side of him, something not many people had seen. He was so like me—kept everything bottled inside and then would crumble. He was such a nice guy and like me, had such a sad upbringing. He had his brother though and in that aspect we differed, as I had never had anybody by my side in my darkest times.

I did have him and Xavier now though and I had to be thankful for that. Hunter had made me feel so welcome here and happy for once in my life and Xavier, as annoying as he could be, was good to have around now. Two aspects I had never had growing up and so seeing him smile again, for however short a time it lasted, was nice and a memory I would forever have to cherish.

I so wanted to relay to him about the training situation and my job offer, but I felt like if I did, he would explode. And I didn't know how many more tears I could handle, so I just sucked up the words for now.

"I bet you are sick of hearing me now. Sorry for crying and all, just couldn't stop it. It's what happens when you let it build up."

"You can cry in front of me any time you like. Let it all out," I laughed.

"Thanks for listening anyhow," he smiled back. "Sorry for burdening you with my troubles, I know you have your own problems to deal with."

"Don't be stupid, I'm here for you anytime. Besides, I always lumber you with mine." I smiled and after a moment of just sitting there in silence, which weirdly didn't feel awkward, he placed his hand on my shoulder, got up, and muttered a *thanks* under his breath as he left.

As much as he seemed to have finally opened up, my smile couldn't help but fade, as I still couldn't help feeling the issue hadn't been resolved. I felt something else was going on inside him. And I would soon find out that just how right my intuition was. I needed to learn to rely on that more.

Twenty-Two

A week and a half had passed since I was offered a job at the company and in that time, I had been putting off replying to them as much as I could. Not because I was still thinking about whether I should take it or not, but because I had an odd feeling that if I declined their offer, something bad would happen. Though I had no idea what that bad thing might be.

For most of my life, I had always had very strong intuition that nine times out of ten wouldn't fail me. As such, I was sticking to that feeling in my gut—the one telling me that this place wasn't right. That it went beyond just white lies. Why would a government supported agency want to help a supernatural without some sort of reward in return? I wished the world worked like that but sadly, I knew there was more to this place and I would soon figure out what it was. I knew people–especially government officials—were only in it for themselves. You see, government officials in today's society were known to be very deceptive and so, I never had a good view of them.

I sat in the training room, getting ready to focus on a board that I had to light up in flames. I honestly didn't see how this helped, but they told me it would teach me to control and balance my brain. To me though, it just seemed like such a waste of time. It was all stupid doing these tasks, since they had told me they were pretty much useless, but I still had no choice but to carry on.

Besides the main speculation about Lucida, my mind had also been lingering with other problems, such as me and Xavier. Since our first kiss, for some reason, I couldn't help but feel awkward around him. I didn't want to see him as I felt so embarrassed because I really did like him, but I had other things more pressing on my mind and so each time he tried to talk to me about it, I would put it off, causing us to bicker. Hunter had still looked off this morning, even though we had talked about it ages ago. I really did hate seeing him like this and I just hoped he would break out of it soon and we could get back to our old ways. I couldn't believe how much I missed the old side of him.

I let out a frustrated sigh after easily completing the task in front of me for once, just wanting them both to get out of my mind. At the same time and just I was about to try out another test when a sudden bout of anger raised from one of the side training rooms, sending a shockwave through me. Hunter's sudden frustrated shouting pierced through the door.

Miri and I gave a look of confusion to each other before she went to investigate the commotion. Hunter had still been in a weird mood since that day I talked to him in my room nearly two weeks ago and he had not really spoken to anyone since then. I had known my intuition had been right and something else was bothering him, more so than just the frustration of his brother. However, I never thought it was a bad enough problem to cause the scene I was about to witness.

Colt and Ben all came rushing out of their practice rooms past me, with their supervisors following behind to see what the commotion was. Ben came and stood by my side as I went over to investigate.

"What is going on?" he asked.

"Don't know, just heard Hunter screaming."

Miri knocked on the door. For the first time since we had met, she looked nervous, as it wasn't one of the rooms with the observation windows and she couldn't see inside. "Alvan, what is going on in there? Is everything alright?"

Silence now lingered on the other side of the door and as Alvan, Hunter's teacher, didn't reply, Miri tried the handle, but it was locked. "Alvan, open the door. Are you okay?" she urged again.

Silence continued for a moment longer, before I heard faint whimpering coming from the other side.

"He's not here," said Hunter in a low tone.

Miri looked at us with concern in her eyes. "Hunter? What do you mean, where is he?"

Suddenly the door unbolted and Hunter presented himself; we stared wide-eyed at the sight of him.

"There he is," he muttered.

The scene that greeted us was ghastly; there was blood splattered all over the floor and there lay Alvan—with a chunk of his head missing.

"Oh my God!" screeched Miri, as she dropped her clipboard and ran to Alvan's side. "What happened?" she demanded, facing Hunter, who just stood there looking shocked.

He gulped, stumbling over his words. "I don't know… I just l-lost control…"

"Is he dead?" queried Ben.

Miri tried to catch his pulse, but after a few moments of trying, nothing came back. "He's dead," she said, trying to fight back tears.

"Oh my God, you killed someone," said Ben.

"It was an accident!" Hunter shouted back. "I just lost control. I told him I wasn't in the right frame of mind, but he kept pushing me and so I threw the chair at him out of anger. It was a moment of rage, an accident…"

"Well, you sure lost your temper alright…"

Hunter caught my gaze and I could tell he was disappointed in himself as well as afraid that he had let his emotions take him over like that. As soon as he saw me, he looked away, seemingly too ashamed to meet my eyes. Which given I had killed people too, I didn't understand.

We all stood there, slightly dazed at what was going on. Hunter had just killed a man. The same guy who had been so nice to me, now was so broken—it was like a different person had taken over his soul.

Guards soon rushed in and dragged Hunter away. "Where are you taking him?" I asked.

A guard only turned his head halfway. "To Daverez," he replied plainly, before dragging him away. I had no idea what that was, but I suspected it was a place to let him calm down, like they had done with Xavier.

Everyone was soon told to go back to the dorms for the rest of the day, which was no surprise. I was the only one to go back straight away though as the others went off somewhere else. As I was walking back to the room, confused and exhausted, Xavier suddenly came running down the hall and grabbed my shoulder.

"Lexia, where is Hunter?" His eyes gleamed with concern and I had never seen so much emotion in his face.

"Uh… I'm not sure," I said nervously as it was the first time we had spoken in a while. "They just took him away to some place called Daverez. I think it's a section of the facility or something."

His eyes widened even more. "Daverez?! Are you kidding? I have to go and get him." And before I knew it, Xavier ran past me, blazing down the hall.

"There is no point, Xavier. They already took him away!" I shouted down the hall, but he ignored me and bolted through the door.

I turned back and began to head back to the common room, just needing a nap as I swear we could never go through one training session without something chaotic happening. Still, never did I think Hunter was the type of person to be able to lose control like that. I didn't realise just how bad he was.

I really did feel sorry for Hunter, but at the moment I had my own problems and frustrations to deal with, so I had to put him to the back of my mind. As I stumbled back into the common room and let out an exhausted sigh, I was just about to get to my room when I suddenly heard Ben calling my name behind me. I turned to see him jogging through the main room into the dorms, seeming a little odder than usual.

"What's wrong?" I enquired as he stopped in front of me and caught his breath.

He didn't speak and for a moment we just stood there, before he looked around as if to make sure we were alone. Before I knew it, he placed his hand over my mouth and pushed me into my room, slamming the door behind him.

Everything that followed happened so fast, my brain had a hard time processing the crazy spectacle. After he slammed my door shut, he pushed me down onto the bed, latching a hand around my neck, pinning down my whole body so I couldn't move. As he stared down at me for a moment, that gaze and smirk sparked something off inside me and from there forth, all hell broke loose.

"Lexia," is all he said in a creepy tone, before proceeding to try and kiss me. I tried my hardest to scream and push him away but even though he was this skinny and lanky guy, he was way stronger than he looked. No amount of punching and scratching seemed to be able to get him away.

As I continued to try and push him away, I could feel the anger in me rising and I knew I was about to lose control. The hairs on my body raised and the heat inside me pulsed through my veins and before I knew it, the whole room around me just blew into a mass of chaos. Then my mind was taken away by the usual cloud of darkness that only appeared when my power showed up, in all of its extremes.

Twenty-Three

I inhaled smoke into my lungs as my eyes suddenly shot open. I felt as if my breathing was going to be cut off at any moment. The whole room was filled with a white fog and the smell of the smoke almost made me choke as it was so potent.

When the smoke slowly started to simmer down, I saw the damage unfold itself in front of me and it wasn't good. My whole room was a mass of crumbled pieces. Fragments broken off in every corner, edges covered with black burns and all my furniture pretty much destroyed. As I tilted my head up to analyse the space further, I saw Ben's body laying across the room, lifeless. Burned to a crisp.

No way. Two killings in one day—could that even be possible?

I stared down at him with widened eyes, before I heard shouting enter the halls and in ran two guards.

"What happened?!" they yelled in unison, before they stopped at the door and observed the disaster zone.

I gulped as they looked at me through narrowed eyes. "Ben attacked me and well, I just lost control."

"Two of these incidents in one day, you have to be kidding." sighed one of the guards, before motioning the other one to come and take me away.

"What will happen?" I urged, my whole body trembling out of shock as they began to drag me away.

"I don't know, it's up to the board to decide."

And with that, I was taken away. I looked back at Ben's body sprawled across the floor, covered in blood, before my own body decided to give up and pass out again.

***

How aren't I dead? was the first thought that went through my mind when my eyelids fluttered open again and I was lying in a bed, still alive. I woke feeling as if I had the world's worst hangover, as my whole body ached with a seething pain that started at my arms. As I pulled them out from under the blanket, I couldn't help but let out a sigh, as the familiar orange tinge was back.

"Oh, great," I groaned in annoyance, flopping my arms back down as it hit me that I had lost control, again.

A voice suddenly croaked from the side of me, confirming my thoughts that I was still alive.

"Lexia, you're awake!" Xavier's shaky tone said from the side of the bed. He looked down at me with concern as he stroked my forehead. More than anything, I was confused to see him act this way. Why did he care about me so much, when we did nothing but fight for most of the time? Why was he always the first person to be there for me? It all made no sense.

"Lexia, what happened? You had me so worried. Especially on top of my brother losing it."

My head ached as I looked at his teary eyes. "It was an accident..." I mumbled through a dry throat.

Xavier sat down on the side of the bed. "You lost control then? But how, was it because of Hunter?"

I shook my head. "No, Ben attacked me and, well—"

Xavier immediately dug his fingers into the thin cotton sheet. "What?!"

"He tried to kiss me and stuff and so, I guess I just lost control when I couldn't break free. It wasn't my fault, I swear—"

Xavier's eyes lookedound the room with anger. "I knew he was a pervert. I'm going to kill the freak."

"I think he is already dead. I don't even know how I'm still alive. The place was a mess—even worse than what I did at college. I've killed someone again, I can't believe it." I cried.

Xavier let out a heavy sigh as his posture calmed down again. "I said I would protect you. I'm sorry I've been so odd with you, it's just everything that has been going on. And with Hunter and all…"

I placed my bruised hand on the side of Xavier's face, seemingly forgetting about the distance I had wanted to create between us. "I understand, I've been odd too. I'm just sick of being here. I think that is why I lost control so much; I've built up so much stress over these weeks that Ben's attack was the breaking point and I finally exploded, just like in college."

He closed his eyes and rested his cheek in my palm. "I won't let it happen again. I'll never leave your side."

I couldn't help but smile as he met my gaze again and I truly believed his words. It was so strange. I didn't understand why I was being so affectionate to the guy I argued with so much and vowed not to have feelings for while I was here, but for some reason, seeing him like this, I just couldn't help it.

Suddenly the thought of what happened to Hunter entered my mind. "How is Hunter?" I said.

Xavier ran a hand through his disheveled hair, seemingly on edge. "He's fine, a little shook up and confused, but he'll be okay. This isn't the first time something crazy like this has happened, you know."

I gave a nod back, knowing he was talking about the police incident.

"So, won't he be arrested? After all, he did kill someone here?"

Xavier shook his head. "No, he is too valuable to lose, so they said they would forgive this one incident. However, he'll have to go and live in another part of the building called Daverez, where there are more apparent supernaturals who have done a lot worse than us. It's not a place I want him to be, I know that much."

A buzzer suddenly went off in my head as he said the last words. "Another part of the facility, other supernaturals, *asset*? Do you mean they have recruited him or something?"

His eyes shifted oddly. "Well, to be honest, I know why this has happened."

"What are you talking about?"

"Why Hunter just lost control like that."

"I thought it was because he was stressed and just lashed out?"

He shook his head. "No, it's something much worse and I should have known it was going to happen." His eyes suddenly started to gleam over.

"Xavier, what are you talking about?" I said with growing concern.

He took a deep breath. "Well, basically, a short while back I was offered a job here, just like you. But refused."

"What?" My eyes widened. "How come you never told me this earlier?"

"Because, it was meaningless to me, so I didn't see the reason to. Besides, you have been keeping a distance from me, so I never had the chance." He cleared his throat and continued, "I guess since I declined, they moved onto him and offered him the job instead. This is what has been troubling him these past weeks."

"Why is he so troubled about this? The offer?"

"Because he has obviously been thinking about it, a lot. If he accepts, then he has to say goodbye to me and that part is obviously what has bothered him most. So he has been trying to distance himself from me, I'm guessing because the offer tempted him. The freedom. The power. The money. The control. I think he felt he was finally going to have meaning in his life, not just be the useless side show that he thinks he is, but he was trying to see if he could cut me off first, before he decided whether to accept."

I couldn't comprehend him ever thinking that way. "That doesn't sound like something he would do, he loves you."

"You're right. It isn't like him. And that is because they have been drugging him and that is how he has lost control so badly. He would never normally hurt a fly, unless there was a good enough reason."

My eyes couldn't help but widen at his words. "Huh? They drugged him?"

Xavier nodded, his expression wrathful. "Yup just like they did with you. Why do you think you have lost control so many times since you were here? Not because you are weak, or because of the harsh treatment or lack of control. They have been drugging you so that you would slowly decline, slowly lose faith in yourself and eventually explode like you have, so that when you come out of it, you'll accept their offer because this unit with its prospects sound so much more tempting when you are weak. In basic terms, they give you a chance to accept. You both didn't do so fast enough and so they now have a reason to take you to the other facility—to help you more, because you're too dangerous."

I shook my head in confusion. "How on earth do you know all of this? That they have been drugging me?"

"Because I watched the surveillance. You know how I sneak around? Well, that explosion I caused weeks ago wasn't just me being stupid. I got mad when I saw what they were starting to do to Hunter, but I had to let it happen because I needed to observe the place. I never thought they would make him kill someone when I didn't agree to join, just so they could get him instead. They are basically using him to get to me. They need reasons to obtain us."

"Oh my God. So, they have been doing the same to me: testing me and drugging me to observe my power in full force, so that they could see what I could truly do?"

He nodded. "From what I have gathered, they didn't want you to kill anyone. However, they've been observing your power, that's for—just waiting for you to *truly* explode so they could bring you here. However, you got mad each time, so they stopped you as you were too strong for them to control, unlike Hunter, whose power is obviously not as good in those stakes. They hadn't found the right moment to get you into the other place, until now."

I clenched my fists, as the thought of what they were doing to me just made my anger want to seep out and destroy the place. "I knew something was up with this place, besides the fact that they weren't using the best training equipment on us. So, they have basically decided that since I haven't accepted their job straight away, they will deliberately try to make me lose it so that they can forcibly take me there. That way, it doesn't look like their fault to their superiors and I am right where they want me, so that they can brainwash me even more into thinking there's hope. No wonder they kept testing me like that. They must be so glad now they finally have a reason to move me there. Though, this drug… What does it actually do?"

"From what I've observed, it makes you stress out, makes every little thing seem more significant. Basically, it makes you go crazy. Everyone reacts differently though; some go crazier than others. I think you took it better than most and still had some handle on yourself."

I let out a deep exhale, still unable to comprehend the severity of this. "I can't believe this. I mean, I knew something was up, but why can't they just urge us to go there without using violence and mind games."

Xavier almost laughed. "Because they want violent people. They want to see you lose it, so they can see what destruction you are truly capable of with their own eyes. That way they know you are worth their time and are capable of their dirty work, even if you don't accept the job. They use your loss of control to their advantage and pretend you are a danger to people when in fact, they make you get worse, instead of better. That is how they are never questioned by the outside monitors—because they make it seem like this is all your own doing."

"I guess that is why my dad left here then. Because the same must have happened to him. No wonder he never told me of this place. It's obviously a hoax to lure in wayward supernaturals who are on the brink of destruction, to observe them before they are thrown into the real thing. If they decide they want them, that is."

"Your dad used to come here?" Xavier said, surprised.

I nodded. "Yeah, Miss. Ellewood told me, but said he ran away. Now I obviously know why. Why didn't I think of him sooner? I wonder if he had any more information about them and what exactly they want us to do in that other facility, given my aunt found the contact number in his old possessions."

Xavier shook his head. "It doesn't matter now, it's all in the past. We need to focus on getting Hunter back."

"You're right, we just need to think of what's happening now."

Xavier nodded. "Anyhow, I'm sorry I never told you sooner. I just wanted to be certain what they were doing. It killed me seeing them drug you guys."

I narrowed my gaze, still confused. "Why don't I remember being drugged anyway?"

"Obviously they erase your memory alongside."

"Great." I huffed.

"I'm going to get my brother back, I just had to make sure you were okay first."

I latched onto his shirt. "Wait, let's think about this. These guys plan this out. We can't just go barging in, as we don't know who could be in this Daverez place. Remember, it's for even worse supernaturals than us by the looks of it."

Xavier nodded. "You're right, I can't let my anger get the better of me. We have to think about this."

"I still haven't replied to them about whether or not I would work here. Maybe I could pretend to say yes, they could take me to live in that unit, and then we could plan our escape route?"

Xavier bit at his lip. "That could put you in danger. They obviously don't want anybody to know about this unit or what it is actually for… They could suss you out and I can't have you in danger."

"If that is the case, why haven't they done anything about you, took you away or made you lose it, given you know about this other place?"

"Because that wouldn't be out of character for me. I lose it all the time, so they have no reason to place me in there yet and just accept my refusal, though I'm sure they are trying to figure out a way for me too. I bet they are crapping themselves since I know about the job and refused. But they aren't acting right away because they know I would blow this place down if they tried to test me. Still, now they have Hunter, that will change. Anyhow, you can't go there alone. It's too dangerous."

I shake my head. "I understand, Xavier, but I can protect myself if it comes to it. I know my control is terrible but we have no choice really. If we just storm in there we have no chance, as we don't know how strong these people are, but if we do it this way then at least I can see Hunter and he can teleport us out. If worst comes to worst, I could use my powers."

Xavier mulled it over for a moment, not really wanting to put me in danger, but knowing we had no other choice. "Okay, but if anything bad happens, I'm coming for you both—no matter what. Anyhow, lucky that Ben guy is dead because I would have killed him if I'd seen him. It's a shame actually, I need to vent some anger."

I gave a nod and silently laughed to myself at his protectiveness. As he pulled me into our first hug, I couldn't help but feel the first momentary blip of happiness I'd felt in a long time. I knew it sadly wouldn't last though and that whatever lay ahead, was not only going to test the deception skills I had built over the years, but also whether I was as strong as I thought. I knew one thing though, they had messed with the wrong supernatural and the true game of lies was about to commence.

***

The next day, the board arrived at my room to tell me my fate. All their faces seemed to be filled with frustration, most likely at the damage I had caused. Then again, it wasn't really even me who created the mess. As I looked at them all gathered around me, it was so hard not to lash out at these liars, but I knew I couldn't as it could put Hunter in danger. As such, I clutched onto the bedsheet as tight as I could, to hold back the anger that raged inside.

"Hello Lexia," said Dr. Lincoln, as he stood by my bed, not looking his usual chirpy self. All I gave was a crooked smile in response, the most I could force at this moment.

He suddenly put his hand on my shoulder, his eyes gazing into mine with fake sympathy. I swear I could see the smirk behind it all; the satisfaction that they had finally gotten me into the weak position they thought they had. "I'm very sorry about what happened yesterday. We knew Ben was a very unsteady young man but we just never thought he would act like that again. Especially when we had told him it was his last chance to prove himself."

I felt a wave of confusion rush through me. "He was unsteady? What do you mean? Aren't we all in here?"

He cleared his throat. "Well, the reason Ben was here was because he had assaulted another young girl and lost control of his power in the process. We gave him a chance after he begged us not to send him to jail and so we foolishly did. Sometimes people just can't be cured, you know. He was a very serious case, one we rarely take on. Unlike you and others, he was incapable of change."

I bit at my lip angrily as I knew what they had done. They hadn't sent him here to try and fix himself—they knew he was far too mentally disturbed, but that is what they wanted. They wanted someone who was going to test me, so I would explode for them, and that is exactly what happened. I was now even more determined to get back at them and it took all my effort not to blow this room up too.

"Oh, I see," I answered through gritted teeth, trying to keep the polite act up, as I still had a chance they might not want me anymore and would just send me to jail.

A question suddenly came into mind though: how on earth had I survived blowing up that place? It was the same with what had happened at college: how didn't I die in all the chaos?

"How is it that I'm still alive, when I caused all that chaos?"

Lincoln smiled. "Some supernaturals are able to use huge amounts of their powers and not get hurt from them. Meaning even if you cause a disaster like that, you can still come out relatively unscathed, as the power lives in your body and essentially it would have killed you by now if it could. It puts a protective layer around you, so that not just your power, but other things can't harm you too."

I gave an understanding nod in reply. Knowing that I could use my power to cause a major incident and not die would come in handy in the future, if I had to make a getaway. I just needed to learn to control it first.

Suddenly he brought me back to reality. "We haven't come here to remind you of the incident, Lexia. You won't need to listen to anything about that if you heed my advice and agree to go along with what we discussed earlier."

"Are you talking about the job offer?" I said.

Lincoln nodded. "Yes, we are very intent on having you join our special unit. However, I'm afraid if you refuse, we will have no choice but to send you to jail as you have caused too many deaths now. So it is your choice, my dear."

I could tell he thought I was going to refuse so when I said, "I'm in" straight away, I could sense his surprise.

"You are?" he said, through widened eyes.

I nodded back. "I have been thinking about it for some time now and I think being around other people like me will be good. Why would I want to go back out into a world where I will never be accepted?" I raised a fake smile.

The board members smiled and Lincoln patted me on the shoulder. "Well, that is great news, Lexia! We are happy to have you on the team."

We all talked about how I would be moving into the new unit soon and what contracts I would need to sign. Just before they left, Dr. Lincoln turned and looked at me with pride, as they finally thought they had gotten me wrapped around their fingers.

I sent him a fake smile back when he left. As soon as they left the room, I dug my nails into the thin cotton blanket, wanting to scream. How dare they think they could use me like this, threatening me with jail. I would get them back and when I did, they would know never to mess with a damaged supernatural like me again.

Twenty-Four

Two days passed before they would let me out of the facility's recovery room and in that time, I had healed pretty well. Apart from the aching headache that seemed to want to linger.

After a groggy start to the morning, we headed to the special unit section of the facility where Hunter now was. I had to admit I was now nervous. This was all happening so fast and I wasn't the best type of person to keep silent on things, therefore keeping this lie to myself would be hard, especially as they were using me in this way. However, I had to get Hunter out of there; I just hoped he would be willing to come with me. These people were good at getting to you and I knew Hunter in his current state of mind would accept any help he could get, as sadly his brain was much weaker than mine and didn't tolerate the drug as well as me.

Before I went into the other facility, I was allowed to say goodbye to Xavier and Colt, who were staying in a special place while they fixed up the dorm room I had blown to smithereens. Xavier and I made sure the plan was still in order before I left, but we kept it secret from Colt as we didn't want to chance him blabbing about something, as he often couldn't hold his tongue. After that, before I knew it, I had arrived at my rather mysterious new dorm.

I was given the lowdown before I entered; the people in this base were *very* advanced supernatural teens who I shouldn't push too far, as they were highly dangerous. This didn't help my nerves at all, as these guys could actually control their abilities and here I was, barely able to light up a tiny flame without killing everyone.

As I entered the unit, I was immediately greeted by four sets of eyes who weren't so impressed to see me and I just knew these people were going to be hard to work with. As I gazed around the room though, I couldn't see the one person I cared about seeing—Hunter. This was sad as I really wanted to talk to him and spew my guts about what the plan was.

As I walked further inside the dorm, I realised it was nothing like the one I had been living in these past few weeks. Ours was so much cosier and a lot more inviting, looked like a government facility from some futuristic sci-fi show. All the walls were painted in slate grey and metal furniture was placed everywhere, even around the TV area. Cameras lay in every corner of the room and along the facing wall as one of the staff guided me to our dorm rooms. I wasn't so keen about having my room facing the common space, but I had no choice in the matter. Also, this group of supernaturals were all wearing weird one-piece grey uniforms with four numbers printed in black down their sleeves; pretty unsightly and not something I looked forward to wearing. Yes, now I understood why they said these people were damaged; why else would you have cameras everywhere other than to watch in case they tried to kill each other.

What I didn't understand though was why they would want such people working for them, if they had to monitor them all the time. I soon realised though: these were going to be the type of people, given the way they glared at me as I walked past them, that would have no trouble in doing exactly what they wanted. Just the type of crazy people you want doing your dirty work.

I ignored their glares as I was shown around my even plainer room. This consisted of a thin metal bed with a cotton sheet thrown on top and a similar built desk and chair at the other side of the room. No windows. Nothing. I didn't have much of a chance to glance at it though as they placed down my bag, then escorted me back into the main lounge to 'greet' everybody.

One of the guards cleared his throat before speaking, his thick Irish accent lingering in the background. "This is your new workmate, Lexia. She has a very great ability and we are happy to have her on the team. Now, why don't you all just get acquainted and we will proceed with training tomorrow."

"Uh, training?" I said confused, as the guards went to me to get on with it so soon.

The man nodded. "Yes, you still have to train. Except this is a lot more intense."

And with that he scuttled out of the room, leaving me to get to know my charming new friends. I knew I would be properly training, I just didn't think it would be so soon.

I gave an awkward smile to the stone-faced group, before one of the eccentric crew finally decided to speak up.

"So, what is this amazing power you apparently have then? More amazing than our last inmate they swapped you for, eh?" said a guy with beaming blue eyes and crazily blonde spiked hair, who was slouched on the sofa looking as if he hadn't a care in the world.

Nice to meet you too, I thought to myself, before putting on a fake smile. "It's nothing amazing, I'm just a Pyrokinetic. And what do you mean, swapped me for?"

A girl with caramel skin and a mass of black hair sat next to the blonde boy. She slanted her head my way before tutting. "That's it? They made us wait around just to find out that is all you can do. They now owe me some hours back."

The spiky-haired guy spoke up again. "Shut up Eva, it's not like you can do anything amazing. Plus, I heard she just blew up one of the units. Is that true? Anyway, the person you're replacing was just this crazy girl who had these two weird sides to her; they were hoping to get her under control but she kept acting up, so they swapped her for you."

I nodded, knowing straight away that they were talking about Dana. I had wondered what had happened to her and now I knew—they had tried to recruit her but decided she was beyond help. "Well, it was an accident, not that I care. Anyhow, this other girl, was her name Dana?"

"Guess that is why you are here then—a person who doesn't care, like us," he replied and everyone raised their brows at me, seemingly impressed by what I had done even though it truly was an accident. "And yeah, her name was Dana. Anyhow, enough about her, she is long gone."

Long gone. I knew straight away what that meant, but I had to retain my composure and not make it look like I cared. "Oh I see. Well, it was either here or the supernatural jail so..."

Suddenly I heard the entrance to the unit clicking open and Hunter walked in looking rather flat-faced as a guard slammed the door behind him. As our gazes met, his face seemed to lighten up for the first time in ages.

"Lexia?" he beamed, as he walked over to me and latched his hands around mine with excitement. "What are you doing here?"

I couldn't help but feel surprised at his response, given I hadn't seen this happy side to him in a while. "Well, pretty much the same reason as you really, something bad happened," I mumbled, feeling slightly awkward.

"So, you are now a part of this unit?" he smiled.

I nodded back. "Yeah, though I don't know how my power is going to be of any use since I'm so useless at controlling it."

Hunter laughed and shook his head. "It doesn't matter, I'm just glad you are here." Seeing him smile again did send a pang of happiness to my heart, but at the same time, confusion, considering all that had just happened.

I dragged him out the earshot of the nosy members. "You suddenly seem more cheerful, what is going on?" I urged.

"I don't know what you mean." he replied.

"Well, you have been pretty depressed this last week and you just killed your trainer. I think that may be two reasons at least?"

He shrugged his shoulders. "Oh, I'm over all that now, it's all in the past. Coming here has made me finally be able to look forward to my future."

"You hate it here," I said.

He beamed a smile that continued to unnerve me. "Not anymore. I now have a new-found hope that I can conquer my power and be one of the best workers in this company. Aren't you excited to do the same?"

I gazed over to the bunch of supernaturals on the sofas, who continued to glare at me. "Well, not exactly."

Hunter slung his arm around my shoulder. "Well, you will be soon. Being here has changed my outlook and I'm sure it will change yours too."

"You only got here yesterday." I said through confused eyes.

"Yes, but like I said, I now know I want to move forward and being here is going to help me do just that."

"What about Xavier, he wants you to leave."

He shrugged his shoulders. "Forget about Xavier, he is a part of a different team now and not our problem. He chose to refuse to work here and wants to go back out into the world that hates us."

I immediately shook away his arm. "How can you say that about your brother?" I shot back.

"Why are you getting so offended? Look, it's better now we are apart then when we are together. It's just a bad mix, for everyone."

This was not Hunter talking. I didn't know what had happened to him in the short time he'd been here,e than I'd thought or more so, they had drugged him with something else that was stronger, which I suspected was the case. It was just the drug making him think like this and I had to stop it.

I couldn't tell Hunter anything now in case he relayed something to the others. As such, I would have to tell Xavier so we could make another plan, otherwise this could all end badly. I just knew I had to see Xavier before they brainwashed me beyond my control also.

Twenty-Five

I woke up the next day still expecting to be in my nice room at the other facility. However, reality soon came crashing down when my eyelids peeled back and I was greeted with the docile grey texture of my depressing new unit. I reminded myself that this was only for a short time. After getting up, I got dressed in the drab prison-like grey uniform that matched the interior of this place, then ate breakfast. I was immediately escorted to go and sign some sort of contract which would make me an official employee of the company.

It was safe to say I was beyond nervous now, which was very unlike me, given I had been through so much in my life. I had gotten used to bad happenings and therefore not much fazed me. However, I'd never dealt with anything like this before—the government or other supernaturals. I couldn't let my nerves show though. I had to go along with everything they said so that they wouldn't be suspicious when I asked to see Xavier, to tell him his brother was even more brainwashed than before. This would be difficult in the first place seeing as they thought we hated each other because of the rows we had.

I was taken to Dr. Lincoln's office and it was still in the disorganised state that it had been when I had arrived weeks ago. His smile had a hint of smugness as he slid a piece of paper across the table that contained the company rules and job details. From training to keeping everything I did a secret when I was sent out on missions into the city.

It all added up to me basically becoming their assassin.

I was never the usual type to let things get to me. However, being surrounded by a group of liars and not yet being able to expose what they were doing was hard, but I had to hold myself back or risk everything because at the end of the day, I didn't know what these people were capable of and although I was strong sometimes, these people were in control and I was not.

I analysed the writing in front of me and saw all the things they wanted me to comply with. From intense training, to the jobs I would be doing for them—such as protecting the company employees and doing jobs for their security in the city when needed. As much as I didn't want to sign my name away, I was going to be storming out of this place soon enough so it wasn't like signing a piece of paper would matter. Soon I would be on their most wanted list and on the run anyway.

I gave a fake smile and signed away my name, Dr. Lincoln beaming one back as I slid over the signed contract.

"Well, I'm so glad to officially have you on board. You'll begin your advanced training soon," he said, just before I headed back to the unit. It all happened so fast that it couldn't help but make me more on edge.

I couldn't believe people would willingly sign away their rights to work for a company that would exploit them, but then again, I didn't know their reasons for being here. However, anywhere seemed better than here and being their slaves. Even though they wanted us to think we were as much a part of this supported government team as them, we weren't. We were just their puppets and I found it sad that these fools couldn't see that. I had to keep remembering what Xavier had said—that they were all drugged and had no choice in the matter.

As I re-entered the facility, I couldn't help but feel a pang of sadness tug at my heart as I didn't see Colt sprawled on the sofa fast asleep or Xavier watching TV with a grumbled expression, ready to attack me with verbal taunts. Instead, it was just my new unit mates, who had as much personality as a dead fish.

Two of them were sitting on the sofas reading about their powers as I walked by. Hunter was nowhere to be seen and just as I was about to head into my room and let out the world's heaviest sigh, a voice called my name from behind, asking me to come and sit with them. As much as I didn't want to, I thought it would be a good idea to get to know the reasons they were here.

As I went to the seating area, the major moody girl and another dark-haired boy were sitting facing me on the sofas. Neither looked my way as I went and sat by the pale lanky guy who had called my name. His black hair was tightly slicked back with so much hairspray that the harsh white lights from above made it glisten. He kept his eyes on his book before he spoke up again.

"How was your contract signing?" he randomly enquired, as I slumped into the seat next to him.

"Uh, good, I guess," I replied plainly.

"Good to know. Well then, welcome to the team." He put down his book and put out his hand. "I'm Adrian Robinson, seventeen, Psychokinetic."

I smiled back and shook his hand, surprised at how suddenly tolerant one person of this group was being, given the lack of a welcoming yesterday. "Lexia Luccen, seventeen, Pyrokinetic."

The side of his lip crooked up into a half smile. "Nice to meet you and yes, I gathered you were a pyro given the explosion you caused, as you told us yesterday. Not many people can do that and *live*," he laughed. "Anyhow, welcome. It may take a while to get settled here, but you should be fine."

He turned his eyes back to his book, but I continued to enquire. "How long have you been here?"

"About seven months now—been a while."

I nodded my head, trying to press for as much information as I could. More so out of curiosity. "I see. So, how have you liked working for Lucida then?"

He shrugged his shoulders, pressing his brown-rimmed glasses closer to his eyes. "It's fine, I guess. Good accommodation, free food—what more do you need? It's, well, a step up from where I lived before I came here, you know."

"I second that," said the young guy with the crazily spiked blonde hair from yesterday as he slumped down in the last empty spot in the couch facing me, next to the moody girl who didn't even budge. "I lived in a freaking mess before I came here and the fact we get all this stuff for free—I couldn't pass up this opportunity." The guy kept a cool expression as he stared over at us, "It certainly didn't help me control my power living in such a place, let me tell you that."

"What power is that?" I enquired.

"Just let's say, I'm pretty strong," he replied bluntly.

I was starting to realise that these people weren't just your typical supernaturals and now I understood why Dr. Lincoln said it was a place for *very* special people. These people were powerful and so I knew now I definitely had to watch them. Especially since they seemed way more in control of themselves than I was right now.

"Super strength then, how cool," I replied, not wanting to sound on edge.

"Yeah, it's pretty neat," he replied, "I'm Conner Hughes by the way. So, what exactly is your reason for being here? Not just for the job, but what brought you to the facility in the first place?" he urged as both his and Adrian's gazes turned to me intently.

An awkward smile raised at my lip. "Well, I kind of blew up my college and killed people when I lost control of my pyrokinesis. It seems to have become a trend in my life as of recent times. Destruction and death." The thought of my dad's death suddenly came into my mind, but I shook him out of my head as the last thing I wanted to do was compare myself to him again. That was something I thought I had buried deep into my brain already.

"Damn," Conner muttered, leaning his chin against his palm. "You'll have to show me what you can do. I mean, I get you can shoot fire and stuff, but I'd love to see a girl use it in person."

I couldn't help but let out a nervous laugh. "I can't. Well, only a small amount, not on the scale that I burned down my college with though or else you'll all be dead too."

Adrian laughed back. "Yeah, we are all here because we lost control big time like you. I think it's because they want people working for them that have no quarrels, in shall we say, doing their *dirty* work."

The three of them started to laugh as he said that and I guessed they had already done some of that *dirty work,* judging by how unfazed they were about all the destruction I had done.

"What sort of tasks have you completed so far then?" I asked.

"Just, you know, like it says in the contract: protect the place when needed be and go out into the city when called," Adrian replied.

"We don't always work in a group, it just depends what they want on the day really, how big the situation is," interjected Conner.

"How big do these situations exactly get? What do you actually set out to do?"

"Mainly kill people," the moody girl from yesterday replied.

Adrian tutted. "No need to spout it out so bluntly, Eva."

"What? She is going to be working here, she may as well know what she is in for. Be prepared to kill, steal and live a used existence. Besides, it's not like she hasn't killed before given what she just said," Eva stated bluntly.

"I agree, she needs to know what happens." said a sudden low tone from behind Eva. As I looked up, I was greeted by the last guy of the group, who I remembered from yesterday as being the only one who hadn't glared at me. In fact, he hadn't even stared in my direction.

"Ignore them, Lexia," Adrian replied through a sigh.

"Only speaking the truth," she said shrugging her shoulders, before getting up and heading into the kitchen.

The other boy took her space, casually leaning back into the couch as he dug his hands into his grey jumpsuit pockets and oddly began smirking at me. His vibe made me feel oddly uncomfortable, but I didn't make it known. Instead, I made sure not to back down and glared my eyes straight into his.

I sat there not knowing what to say. My worst fears had been confirmed: this place was like an assassin's lair or something, a place they could train powerful beings to do their work for them without having to lift a finger. Also, this place might be even harder to escape from then I realised.

"It's not as crazy as she makes it sound. We only do tasks like that once in a blue moon, we mainly just try and hack into systems and what not," Conner said. "And for that we have Lucas Denver over there, who does most of those tasks, even though that isn't his main power. Anyhow, we hardly do much, sadly."

I turned my head to face back to Lucas once he'd finished, who was still annoyingly smirking at me. "So, what is it you do exactly, Lucas?" I said with a raised brow.

He slanted his head slightly, as if to observe me more with his striking, almond-shaped dark brown eyes. "I can do two things, really. Though I wouldn't call hacking systems a power, just knowledge. My true power is just like yours."

"Huh?"

"I'm a Pyro, too."

My mouth gaped a little, not just with shock but also with excitement at the fact I had met someone similar to me. "You are a ... Pyrokinetic?"

He nodded. "Yeah, pretty similar now, aren't we."

"How come none of you told me?" I urged, gazing around the

room towards the others.

Conner shrugged his shoulders. "Never really thought about it. Besides, we had just met."

I suppose it wasn't that surprising, given that they were used to being around supernaturals, but for me, I was still a newbie in this field. Of being so open about this side of me.

"So, can you control your ability well?" I enquired.

Lucas nodded. "Yeah, otherwise I wouldn't be in this company, would I?"

"I have no control, but I'm here."

"Yes, you're still new though. I have been here for two years so it would be weird if I couldn't, considering how much training I've had."

"I see. Must be nice to have control over this horrendous power."

"I'll be happy to show you sometime, maybe I can teach you how I learned to control it. You might learn faster if someone with the same power helps you," he said through another smirk that oddly reminded me of Xavier. I inwardly recoiled with hatred at the thought I was comparing them both.

I smiled with way too much enthusiasm, given that I wasn't really here to train anymore, but rather to save Hunter. I still kept up the lie though. "That would be great, anything is worth a try."

He nodded back and smiled before turning his gaze back to a book he had picked up. I couldn't help but feel a sense of odd happiness at the fact I had met someone similar to me, who might be able to help me. Who, firstly, was not my father and second, actually had control over this power. But I had to make sure I didn't forget my plan and get lost in this place, especially as it was so tempting to learn how to control this power.

I needed to see Xavier and *soon*

Twenty-Six

The next day, after my mild bonding session with the group, I begun to put my plan into action.

I decided to ask Dr. Lincoln if I could go and see my old roommates and I couldn't believe it when he agreed for one last time. Soon I wouldn't be allowed to because my new training had to become my priority. It was a good sign too, that even though I had been here a short time, I hadn't blown my cover yet and they were yet to suspect me.

Just before I left Dr. Lincoln's office, the sudden realisation of what my aunt would think about me working here suddenly entered my mind. I turned to face him again as I stood in the doorway, his eyes looking up at me with surprise. "Dr. Lincoln, I was just wondering... Does my aunt know about my job here now and that I will be living here on a permanent basis?"

The question seemed to catch him off guard a little, but he still managed to raise a smile as he pushed back his glasses and looked up at me from his desk. "Of course she knows, we have been sure to call her, don't worry."

I didn't believe his words at all. I could tell he hadn't informed her and I didn't think he ever would. I gave an understanding nod in response, before heading down the halls to another unit that the final members of my old group were staying in, as I had practically obliterated our old facility. I couldn't help but wonder why they wouldn't tell my aunt, as it wasn't like it would look bad to her. I was sure she would be happy to have me away from home more permanently, thinking I was doing well. Something didn't sit well with me and I had a bad feeling something had happened to her.

I brushed off the thought for now, however, as I had enough going on. I focused on the problem at hand because I knew I had to use this time wisely with Xavier, given that I might not see him again for a while.

After walking down the all too familiar corridors with a guard accompanying me to get me through the checkpoints, I arrived at the small unit near a part of the building I had never been before. As I opened the door and entered into the unit, the guard telling me to be quick, I gazed around at the new space and it was nothing like our old place. I couldn't help but feel a stab of guilt at the fact they had to live in an all-white sterile-looking plain room with nothing but some odd couches, a TV, and some small bookshelves. Then again, it was not my fault I had been attacked.

I walked through the small square room, my eyes drifting back to the couches as I saw Xavier sprawled on one of them asleep. I couldn't help but smile as I went and sat by him on the sofa; he looked so cute when he slept, his curls laying over his sun-kissed skin so delicately.

I stroked the side of his face gently and couldn't help but admire how peaceful he looked. It felt so strange being near to him again, given I had tried to avoid being close since the day we kissed. He had tried to talk to me about what our relationship was, but I just had put it off each time, scared it would interfere with my life. However, now that was no longer a problem, I decided that when this was all over, I would talk to him about it. Because going through this, I realized just how much he meant to me. I so did want to wake him up, but he looked so serene that I couldn't. Luckily I didn't have to, as Colt's voice boomed into the room, sending us both into shock.

"Lexia, what are you doing here?!" Colt said as he walked over and wrapped me into a hug. This caught me by surprise, given I had seen him not long ago, but I still appreciated the gesture. I smiled as he did so though, glad to know we were finally back on good terms.

"I came to ask Xavier something," I said, just as Xavier looked up with groggy eyes, seemingly surprised to see me sitting next to him.

"Lexia, what's up?" he yawned, sitting up on the sofa to face me.

I looked up at Colt for a second, who seemed to get the drift that I wanted to talk in private. He gave a little wave goodbye before retreating into his room.

"I had to come and see you about Hunter," I said.

"What's been happening?" he asked.

I swallowed, knowing that the words I was about to spew would rile him up. The fact that anyone had tampered with Hunter again could easily be enough to send him on a killing spree, I could just see it, so I had to choose my words wisely. "Well, he's seemingly changed overnight."

Xavier immediately broke out of his groggy state, narrowing his eyes. "What do you mean, *changed*?" he enquired bluntly, clenching his jaw as he sensed I was about to relay bad news.

I bit at my lip. "Well, I'm not certain but he seems to have been brainwashed somehow. He was odd and said to me that you are now in the past and that he wants to stay in the unit. I knew something was up because I know how close you two are. He couldn't have just magically changed overnight."

"You're right. He would never say something like that willingly, something has happened and I think I know what."

My eyebrows raised. "What do you mean?"

"Well, you know how I often escaped the facility? Well, I would sometimes look around and one day I came across this odd room with loads of metal beds laying in a line. On each side, there were these medicines."

"What kind of medicines?"

"Well, that's the thing. I overheard someone say 'get the eraser' once, but I kind of forgot about it. The thing is, they took Hunter to that room before he entered the unit the other day, but they made me leave before I could see what happened as they injected him. That stuff must be a memory eraser or something. They've given him another drug that I wasn't aware of."

My posture straightened at the thought. "Oh my God, you think they erased part of his memory?"

He shrugged his shoulders. "I think so, given they have been drugging you guys with those mind-altering pills. If they have there will be hell to pay, because I won't let them hurt him again. I will blow this damn place up. Now I think about it—you remember when you told me about the conversation you overheard in the waiting room? Well, that confirms my suspicions even more."

"Oh yeah. But, you had told me to ignore it back then."

"Yes, because I was keeping everything silent, wasn't I. The fact they drugged you guys and all."

"I see. If this is true and they have done that to him, what are we going to do? I don't think I can tell him about our plan because of the way he was acting. I think he would tell the staff and I certainly don't want my memory erased."

Xavier bit at his lip, contemplating what course of action to take. "Yeah, don't say anything just yet. I have an idea though: I'll make a scene and break through the door and you get everyone to run out. I'll then lock us inside and explain all. He'll have to listen to me and if he doesn't, then we'll have no choice but to escape. Because I'm not having them dilute my brother's brain anymore. I'd rather die."

I latched my hands onto his. "This could be dangerous though, Xavier. The guys in that unit are no joke, they're really powerful and well-trained. And if anything were to happen, how could I possibly help when I can barely control myself? If I exploded, you would all die."

Xavier smiled, his grip tightening around mine. "Don't worry about that, I can take down any idiot that messes with us. Especially when they touch my family or if they dared to touch you."

"Do you think they really have brainwashed him though? Maybe I am just looking too much into this and he has had a change of heart?"

Xavier laughed. "Trust me, I already had my suspicions just before he entered the unit. He was terrified and still depressed, he can't suddenly have had such a drastic change of heart and be so upbeat. I know him too well."

I gave an understanding nod. "So, when should we execute this plan?"

"Today," he simply stated.

"Can I help?" Colt interjected, walking into the room with his eyes beaming with an odd determination.

"Colt, you were listening?" I said in annoyance as he came and stood by me.

He shrugged. "I can't believe you never told me you had such a plan. If this is true, I don't want to be here. Let me help, too."

Xavier and I exchanged glances, but we knew having his power on board would be a great asset, even if he couldn't control it. Something was better than nothing.

I gave a nod. "Fine, you understand the plan?"

"You distract, we lock him up. I get it. This is so exciting."

I rolled my eyes and then we decided Colt would go along and help Xavier, giving him back up when he blew open the door.

And so, after hugging Xavier goodbye, I headed back to the unit, where I would wait at the sofas for him to blow the doors down and project *Save Hunter* would begin. Even though it was going faster than I'd have liked, the faster we got out of this place, the better. I didn't want to lose any more control over myself than I already had, and I knew brainwashing would mean just that. Even if my past was full of pain, I was not going to let someone else control my destiny.

Twenty-Seven

As I arrived back at the facility, everybody was sat at their usual spaces on the sofas. I analysed them all just lounging there for a moment, so that when it was time to attack; I would remember whose powers were whose. I sat by my fellow pyrokinetic mate Lucas, whose eyes were firmly fixed on a soap opera repeat on the television. I really wanted to get to know him more, as I thought he would help me learn to control my abilities, but sadly today could be the last day we even sat in the same place. And although I had only known him for a day, it was still sad we couldn't have gotten to know each other further, as finding someone with the same ability as you was very rare indeed.

As I turned my head to look at him, our gazes met. A smirk pulled up his lip but I internally brushed it off as I really wanted to learn more about his powers and how he controlled them while I had some time left.

"So, Lucas," I began, as the awkward smile continued to raise at the corner of his mouth, "how long did it take you to gain control over your Pyrokinesis?"

He let out a soft sigh at my question, his mouth straightening as he turned his head back to face the T.V., seemingly disappointed I hadn't asked something cruder, given the way he had kept gazing at me. "About a year to gain full control." The corner of his mouth lifted again as he turned back to face me. "It wasn't easy, let me tell you that—especially when you have anger issues like me."

My eyebrows raised at his last words. "You have anger issues?"

He nodded. "Yes, why else would I have been brought to this facility in the first place? We all have anger issues here on some level. Don't you?"

I nodded back. "Yes, I do. That is the main reason I find my ability difficult—it mostly only seems to want to come out in huge amounts when I get angry, defensive or stressed. And since that is how I generally feel ninety-nine percent of the time, it isn't easy."

Lucas placed his hand on my thigh. "That is exactly how I used to be. If you just keep training the way they tell you to, I'm sure you will get there in no time. It isn't easy though, I must admit."

I narrowed my eyes and brushed away his hand off my leg, his smile not fading in the slightest as I did so. However, his words were more so on my mind and judging by them, there was some hope left for me. And although I probably wouldn't be doing the training here because we would be escaping, at least I knew there *was* hope and I could take some of methods they had taught me on board. I couldn't help but smile slightly at the thought of not becoming my father.

As my eyes glanced around the room and Hunter entered my mind, I sighed with relief as I saw him lounging on a sofa next to a bookshelf. He even looked different; he was normally a casual guy yet now he sat so formally with his legs crossed. It almost made me cringe. He couldn't be the same person.

I rested my chin against my palm and let out a sigh of exhaustion at the thought of how coming here was supposed to help me learn to control my anger and my abilities. I'd had so much determination when I first came here that I was convinced I'd leave a changed person; no more thoughts of becoming like my useless dad. And as happy as I had felt a second ago at what Lucas had just said, I still couldn't help but think I was never going to gain control. However, that now wasn't going to happen here for sure, as the metal doors of the entryway swung open behind me, making me startled. Dr. Lincoln walked in with a group of guards and I just knowing something bad was about to commence as I turned my head to face the gloomy crowd arriving. The group looked up in confusion at the sight suddenly surrounding us.

"What's going on?" Adrian asked, as Lincoln came over and placed his hand on my shoulder, sending a shudder down my spine with his cold and forceful touch.

"We have a traitor in our midst," he said.

The group immediately darted their eyes to me, even Hunter looking up from his book in confusion.

"What do you mean?" enquired Lucas, as he shifted his head to face Dr. Lincoln.

Dr. Lincoln smiled. "I mean, this girl here," he urged, tapping me on the shoulder, "has tried to deceive us, alongside two other members of the other facility. What they don't realise is that we have eyes and ears all over this place and heard their little plan of trying to escape with Hunter over there. But we can't let you do that, can we, Miss Luccen?"

He sent a cold gaze to me and I couldn't help but gulp.

"Lexia, is this true?" asked Lucas, his gaze filled with concern as he latched his cold hand onto my arm.

I didn't know what to say as all eyes stuck onto mine, as this could be the end of me and being surrounded by all of these strong and able supernaturals, I knew I stood no chance.

"Of course it's true, isn't it, Ben?" said Dr. Lincoln, the familiar name sending a shudder through my body as he uttered it. And as I turned to my left, I saw the guy who had jumped me only a short time back and whom I thought I'd killed, walking casually into the room, a confident smile curling at the side of his lip as our eyes met.

"This is Ben, everybody—the little spy we use," Dr. Lincoln beamed, walking over to Ben and placing his arm around him. "If anybody enters the other facility and we don't trust them, we send Ben here into the place, so we can weed them out. And while observing, you found out some very interesting things, didn't you, Ben?"

"Very interesting indeed. Especially during the last forty-eight hours, when I overheard the conversation they had about talking to Hunter before trying to leave," said Ben, looking pleased with himself.

"Now we couldn't have that, could we?" replied Dr. Lincoln.

"How are you alive?" I asked through widened eyes.

Ben smiled. "It wasn't that bad. I'm pretty strong, you know."

"So, I'm guessing what they told us about you is a lie?" I spat, clenching my fists, my fear fizzling out now at the fact they had been watching me for even longer than I had realised.

"Not all of it," he smiled. "My power is self-protection and sensitive hearing, so a little shock like the one you gave me wouldn't hurt me.

As Ben and I stared each other down, the group stared at me with disbelief.

"Why would you lie and want to escape, Lexia? This facility is here to help people like us!" Adrian shouted suddenly, a frown creasing at his forehead.

I'd had enough and jumped up from my seat. "I haven't lied per se, I have stated from day one that I never wanted to be here and that I've only stayed because I knew I needed help. But they aren't helping. Don't be so foolish, you have all been brainwashed and I know it will be me next—that is why I want to leave this place!"

"So, it's true," said Lucas, jumping up next to me.

"Look, it's not what you think," I lied, trying to think of something to divert the tension away from me.

"Oh, it truly is and you have been busted, you traitor. I heard all of your conversations with Xavier and they were very revealing about you both," Ben said, smirking.

"You pig..." I spouted angrily.

"Enough of this!" interjected Dr. Lincoln. "Now, Lexia, you can either come with me, with ease, or go the hard way. What shall it be?"

As I looked at the guards who were holding injections ready to stab me, and the realisation I was surrounded by strong supernaturals dawned on me, I knew I had no other choice but to give in. However, this was something I would never do.

"I haven't done anything wrong, you used me, but I will come quietly," I grumbled.

I was just about to make a break for it, as the guards moved forward to me on Dr. Lincoln's nod, but suddenly there was a sizzling sound from behind them and everyone turned to face the entrance as a blue light shone through the cracks. Soon, Xavier and Colt burst into the room, as Xavier used his electricity to burn open the door.

He looked ready to fight as he stormed inside, but as he locked gazes with Dr. Lincoln, his posture straightened.

"What is going on?" Xavier enquired in surprise. However, before we could even make an attempt to snatch Hunter and run for it, we were frozen in place and injected with a solution that moments later, made my mind fade into a dark haze.

Twenty-Eight

As I woke up, my vision was surrounded by a film of fog. It took what felt like an eternity before it slowly started to dissipate, eventually allowing me to see again.

My whole body was throbbing with an aching sting that was reminiscent of the last time I had been stabbed in the neck with the same solution. And as I tried to move my arms to slowly lift myself up, it took all my energy not to fall straight back down onto my back, as the pain was so intense. As I managed to sit on the edge of the metal bed, my vision started to clear and I slowly began to realise I was in a room I didn't recognise.

It was all white, with four metal beds in a row. As I turned to look down at the row, I noted that hanging on each side of them was a drip bag filled with some clear liquid. I quickly looked down to my arms and sighed with relief as I made sure I wasn't attached to any strange machine. However, as my mind started to focus as much as it could, I gazed around to find I was the only one in the rectangular stretch and the others—who had also been stabbed with a shot—were nowhere to be seen. That was when the panic began to set in, and it somehow managed to override the aching of my body.

I gathered whatever energy I could and headed to the door to my left of the bed, which had a small window in the middle of it. I stared frantically out into the hall, but it was desolate. I sat back down on the edge of the bed and contemplated my options, the pain no longer at the forefront of my mind.

What options of escape did I have? I could blow the door open, but that would require some control, something which I didn't have. As such, I could end up blowing the entire place up with us still inside. Option two: I could somehow break the glass on the door and unlock it from the outside—melting it maybe. However, once again, control was the problem.

I let out a sigh full of frustration, trying to conjure up an escape plan. However, there was soon no need to bother, as the door clicked open and in walked a guard with a gloomy, slightly withered expression on his face. He gestured for me to follow him out and I abided by the rules, as I needed to see what was going on, so I could attempt to put something into plan.

The guard led me down one of the gleaming white hallways, before we stopped at a double door. After tapping in a pin number, we entered and I looked around another new space that was filled to the brim with people. It was a large hall with high ceilings and an exterior that matched the white I knew all too well. It was also completely empty of any furniture or objects aside from the people soon holding my gaze as I entered.

I saw my group members sitting in the left corner of the room on the floor with poker faces, their eyes widening as they saw me. Dr. Lincoln and an array of guards and boardroom members all stood in a line, just watching me enter with stone cold expressions that made my spine straighten with nerves.

As my eyes narrowed in onto the scene at hand, Colt and Xavier in the corner of the room; Colt was sitting with a strange white device wrapped around his head whilst Xavier was sitting slumped against the wall next to him, the same kind of device wrapped around his hands. Anger immediately ran through me as I saw them and as I looked at Hunter just standing there idly with his new group, I just knew he had been brainwashed.

"What's going on?" I urged through clenched fists, as I could feel my anger starting to rise from seeing Xavier look so helpless.

Dr. Lincoln motioned for the guard behind me to shut the door and he obeyed, disappeared into the hall as he did so. I turned back to face Dr. Lincoln, whose gaze began to gleam.

"Took you long enough to wake up, dear. Anyhow, look at your friends Lexia, what do you think is happening?" replied Dr. Lincoln, looking smug.

"What have you done to them?" I said, my blood boiling at every word that left his mouth.

"Nothing too concerning, as of yet." he said, beginning to walk over to Xavier and Colt. "We have just temporarily stopped their powers, so they don't go crazy while we fix this situation. We really don't want to have to kill any of you, given your powers would be a great asset to our company. However, if we must, since you won't work for us, then I'm afraid we have to consider the option."

"I'll fix this situation for you, shall I?" I spat, not knowing if it was me or my anger moving me forward to hit him. Dr. Lincoln flicked his hand in the air and Adrian stepped forward and sent me flying back to the ground. As I lay a slumped out mess on the floor, my arm seething with pain from where it had taken the impact upon falling, Adrian extended his hand and crushed his pale palm tightly together. As he did so, my lungs slowly began to shut down.

"I'll kill you!" Shouted Xavier, as he tried to break free from the cuffs to stop Adrian. Colt simultaneously tried to mumble a curse in the background, but he failed because of the equipment they were wearing. Adrian didn't even flinch as he continued to take away each breath from me.

I could feel myself slip away again, into the dreamy hazed-out state that I seemed to know so well since coming here. It was like a rope was being pulled tighter and tighter around my airwaves and as the oxygen continued to be sucked out of my lungs, Xavier's pleas in the background started to be drowned out as my senses shut down. Before I knew it, my mind started to fade away into my past for some reason—to a memory that had started off the trail of destruction in my life. The moment that truly made me see the word *control* was not in my vocabulary and never had been in my life.

Twenty-Nine

I was transported back to a memory of when I was eight years old. The memory that had first noted to me in my mind that I was different. It was also the first time that I had ever used my ability to such an extent that I realised I was slowly becoming a monster.

I was sitting by myself in the school playground, like I usually did, when a group of girls from my class came and started to annoy me. It was always over the same thing: my mother and father and the state they were in. They were drunks and often took me to school looking a mess, so people started to bully me when they saw how wild they were, tarring me with the same brush.

It was the first time I used my power to create more than just a light spark and the first time I truly saw a change in myself. It was as the girls stood there, mocking me, that something inside me just ticked away and I knew that at any moment, my power would unleash and injure everyone around me. Almost killing some in the process. It was the first time I had experienced near death and was the reason, that when I killed those girls at college, it didn't bother me as much as it should have. The only thing that did was the fact I had lost control like my father. And what happened that day, when I was eight years old, was ultimately the reason my mother took her own life, as she couldn't bear the thought of what I had done. The monster she had brought into this world had almost killed and showed no remorse for it.

I didn't enjoy hurting others. I hated it. But, there was nothing I could do. My power controlled me and since my father didn't guide me, then obviously it would happen again and again. As such, I become immune to the pain hurting people caused.

It was the first real time I realised how strong my power was, as I saw the uncontrollable force shoot out of my body and send everyone flying around the yard in a smoky blaze. There were screams and cries of 'witch' as they went and told on me, but of course, no one believed them.

That memory had stuck with me throughout my life because it was the one that started off a chain reaction of bad events that spanned out in my future. I have never truly been the same since.

After the images of my past continued to reel by like a mental movie of my past life, I felt my mind slipping further and further away. However, just before it could suddenly end, it shot back into the room and I heard Xavier's pleads once again, making me gasp for air as I arrived back into the space.

"Stop it, I'll freaking kill you!" Xavier yelled, trying to break free.

I turned my head to see that Eva had moved closer towards me and as I saw the light return to Eva's gaze and a smirk curl at her lip, Dr. Lincoln came and kneeled beside me. "You see, Lexia. Worse than this will happen if you refuse to comply. Now, I'm going to give you and your friends one last chance, because I truly believe you will be an asset to our company. You either join or you die."

In that moment, I would have loved to have slapped the smile off his face, but instead, I spit words at him. "I'd rather bleed to death, you damn pig," I smiled back through gritted teeth.

He immediately stood and ignored my reply, ushering the guards to bring over Colt and Xavier to sit next to me in the middle of the room. Xavier was thrown down beside me and he latched onto me as much as he could through the machine tied around his wrists. For the first time, I could see his face was muddled with sadness.

Dr. Lincoln went and whispered to a disinterested Lucas, who was leaning casually against the wall with his hands in his pockets. However, after they finished speaking, he started walking towards me, his face emotionless. *This is a shame*, was all I could think to myself as my breathing tried to steady. I would have loved to have gotten to know him—the first person I had met with a similar ability to mine who could actually control his power. It's sad he had been brainwashed to work here.

He looked down at me, tilted his head and just when I thought he was about to attack me, he suddenly turned towards Xavier, whose face was blaring with anger. However, that rapidly diminished when his tied hands gravitated towards his throat; Adrian, not Lucas, had suddenly opened his other hand up, stopping Xavier's breathing. Xavier heaved and heaved, trying to catch his breath, but there was nothing he could do. Lucas was oddly motionless, staring at me like he couldn't do anything.

"Stop it!" I yelled, just about to get up, but I was automatically flung back down to the ground by Adrian's hand.

Colt froze to the ground, trying to figure out what to do, his gaze frantically shifting around the room, but we no longer could move and as Xavier's face turned blue, my heartbeat picked up as the panic began to set in. "Please stop, I'll do anything!" I yelled.

And suddenly he did. Xavier caught his breath and slowly began to calm down as his breathing returned like mine. Lucas returned back to the line, seemingly confused with himself, as Dr. Lincoln walked forward and kneeled in front of me again.

"You will do anything?" he repeated. I bit at my lip, not wanting to waste my own energy on him, but I couldn't let him win and gave a nod in response.

"Then I will give you one last chance. Join the company willingly or be forced to; it's all up to you, Lexia. I just want you to choose the first option."

I stared at Xavier and Colt, then at Hunter, and I knew I had no choice but to agree. "Fine. I'll join," I replied.

"Lexia, you can't!" shouted Colt.

Of course I didn't want to, but it was the only way I could get out of this situation. I needed to get away from this strong group and play for time until they were separate. At least then, if I was attacking them individually, I had a chance of winning. It wasn't a definite—but I had to try.

"I'll do it," I repeated to Dr. Lincoln, sending a stern gaze his way.

A smile curled at his lip. "Well then, for the second time, welcome!" he beamed, clapping his hands together before whispering in my ear. "The only thing is, if you try another thing like this, then an injection will go into your neck and you will have no choice but to work here then. Do I make myself clear? This is your last chance—take it and you will never have to become like the other brainwashed idiots, okay. Besides, you don't want to become your father, do you?" He thought the 'father' remark would annoy me, but it no longer did. I wasn't him and I knew that now. As such, I gave a fake understanding nod as he got up. "Now, let's get back to normality, shall we? Guards, take away these two. Group, return Lexia back to the unit."

"Wait, why can't those two join?" I said.

"They aren't what we are looking for in this team, I'm afraid, as I know they won't conform like you. However, you still have something left to work with." And with that, he disappeared into the hall, his army following behind him.

Two guards lifted me by the arms and started dragging me away and as I heard Xavier's yelling in the background, I couldn't help but feel emotional at how there was nothing I could do. It was so strange to be in this situation. I wanted to save someone. Me, the girl who had killed so many people, wanted to now save people—something I never thought I'd feel.

However, as I felt a hand grip around my waist that didn't belong to the guards, the thought soon fluttered away and before I knew it, I was drifting through some sort of wind tunnel that was very familiar.

Thirty

As my body landed with a thump on the floor, I lay on the ground, having no clue what had just happened. However, as a memorable sickly feeling churned in my stomach and I realised that I had face-planted with the floor, my head whipped around to see if the familiar feeling was what I suspected. As I did this, I saw Hunter standing there looking as confused as me.

"Why did I just do that?" he said, his face completely drained of colour as he began frantically pacing around behind me.

"What just happened Hunter?" I urged back, as I stumbled up and tried to analyse the situation more.

He looked panic-stricken as his gaze staredto, but at the same time, I'm going to be in so much trouble." He huffed, beads of sweat beginning to form on his brow.

I took a deep breath at the realization he had tried to save me, but he couldn't figure out why because he had been brainwashed. I went over and put my hands on his shoulders, trying to calm him down. "Hunter, take it easy. It's because you're my friend—that is why you saved me. They have brainwashed you and that is why you feel guilty, but the real you wouldn't have. Trust me."

I saw a glimmer of familiarity shine in his eyes as our gazes met. "Brainwashed?" he mumbled.

I nodded.

"Why would they do that to me, they said they were here to help?" he replied, evidently his mind still not fully taken over by whatever they had done to him.

I shook my head back. "They want to use us—that is why. And that is why this is all happening, because I want to get you and your brother out of here."

As Xavier suddenly entered my mind, I turned around to scan the hall we had landed in, but soon realised he was nowhere to be seen around us, nor was Colt. "Didn't you bring Xavier too?" I urged, feeling the panic begin to set in.

He shook his head. "No, I just thought of you and then for some reason leaped forward and teleported. I've never done that so fast before."

"Oh my God," I groaned, gripping my hands through my hair in a panic. "We have to go and get them; quickly, teleport us back."

"I can't, I'm too stressed now. It won't come to me that quick."

I narrowed my eyes at him and couldn't stop myself from getting angry, even though I knew it wasn't truly him talking to me. "Great, if we don't get them now, they may kill them or worse, brainwash them. I have to get back there."

Just as I was turning to find a way back, Hunter grabbed me by the shoulders. "You can't go back now, they will lock us away!" he pleaded.

I shook his hands away. "Hunter, Xavier is your brother, you care about him so much, the real you does anyway. We have to go save him and Colt!"

He gazed at me for a moment, before letting out a sigh. "Fine, I will try and teleport." For a moment he just stood there, trying his hardest, but his power refused to come through. "I can't, I'm sorry."

I let out a sigh myself this time. "It doesn't matter, we just have to get them and then get out of here, okay? Now, let's go."

We ran out of the hall we had landed in and peeked our heads through the doors—which oddly had no checkpoints—hoping we could find our way back, even though we had no idea if they would still be there. I had no idea what part of the building I was even in, as everything looked the same in these gleaming white halls, so it was hard not to get lost. However, I just had to try everywhere, even though there was a possibility I would be attacked in the process. I had to fight and if worst came to worst, I had so much anger in me already, I would just have to conjure up my power and destroy this place, so nobody else would have to go through this web of lies again.

As we were running through the halls, I suddenly heard footsteps approaching us from around a bend, so I quickly dragged Hunter into a side room and hid there, waiting for whoever it was to pass.

As the footsteps thankfully passed and my heartbeat lightened, I turned to see what room I was in and as I did so, I saw a familiar face lying on a metal bed, making me gasp.

Elisa, the moody girl I had first met upon arrival at the facility and who had supposedly left weeks back, was lying on a metal bed in the middle of the room, a drip attached to her arm and restraints placed all around her body. Looking lifeless.

"Elisa?" I whispered out of confusion, as I slowly stepped towards her. At first, her eyes didn't move, but as my shadow moved in front of her, they slowly peeled back and revealed something shocking.

"What happened to your eyes?" I said. She just stared at me for a moment, the whites of her eyes bright red and the shade was slowly turning black.

"Lexia?" she uttered weakly under her breath. "What are you doing here?"

"I could ask you the same thing. I thought you had left?"

Suddenly, panic filled her gaze and her cold palm latched onto my arm. "Lexia..." she urged through a cough, "you ... you all have to get out of here... They are lying..."

"I know, that's what we are doing now. You'll never believe all the stuff that is going on right now." I placed my hand on hers, trying to calm her down.

"Lucida... They don't want to help us, they want to use us. You have to get out of here... all of you!" She nearly screamed the words now, her voice hoarse with exhaustion.

"Look, I know all of this, Elisa. I'll help you get out of here. Just let me..."

"No!" she shouted, shaking my arm. "It's too late, I'm almost wiped out... Just get everybody and leave now or your memory will be wiped away too and then they will force you to work here..."

"So, they really do try and take your memory then?" I said, looking up at Hunter.

"Yes. They are training us up and then wiping away our memory and emotions, so we can become their weapons. If we say no to joining the company, this is what happens.. I'm not the only one. You have to get out of here now, while you still have hope…"

"They asked you to join the company too?" I enquired, confused.

"Yes, but I said no and that is why I'm here. Because they want my power regardless of whether I agree or not and the same will happen to you if you don't leave. So, go now! Or they'll kill you just like me and that other girl!" she yelled.

"Are you talking about, Dana? And, they are killing you right now..."

"Yeah, she wouldn't join and so they killed her, sucking up her power first like what they are doing to me here. I'm next because I don't want to join either." She suddenly turned her gaze to Hunter. "Hunter, get her out of here—all of you have to leave. Go!"

"I can't leave you here, they are killing you. Come on Elisa, come with us!" I urged.

She pushed my arm away, as we heard footsteps suddenly emerge in the hall. "Lexia, get out of here! You have a chance, you must leave and tell the world about what Lucida is doing! They are taking damaged supernatural youth and using their weak self-esteem or their crimes against them. Pretending to train them, when in fact, they are just wasting time so they can recruit them when they feel useless. If they don't want to join, well, then it's goodbye. Whether that be mentally or dead, it depends on how they feel about you. You have to tell the world."

As the footsteps got closer and closer, I took one last look at Elisa. "I'll be back," I said to her. Hunter and I headed out a side door, running even faster to get to the others, to stop them becoming Lucida's zombies. Or end up dead if they didn't want me after all. This was no longer a game but a battle commencing.

Thirty-One

As Hunter and I stormed through the halls, I felt a mixture of worry and anger. A cocktail that doesn't mix well with my power and so I had to be careful not let it rise too far, until I had found them at least. Xavier would have been the type to have blown up the place by now, but since he was strapped onto some power control gadgets, he couldn't. And for the first time, I was actually glad he was, as he wouldn't destroy the place before we had a chance to escape.

As we were searching down the halls, I suddenly came across a set of familiar doors and heard the voices of the other unit inside. I gave an agreeing look to Hunter, who truly didn't know what to do, but as I burst inside, I saw nothing but the group talking in a circle. Xavier and Colt were nowhere to be seen.

"Where are they?" I yelled, trying to keep calm and as they all turned around, I couldn't help but gulp, as I was way outnumbered and couldn't be sure if Hunter would back me up, considering he had no idea what side to truly pick yet.

"Somewhere they will be looked after," smirked Eva, which made me feel the fire begin to prickle with annoyance at my fingertips. Thankfully, I managed to suppress it.

I let out a deep breath, remembering to keep myself calm so I didn't go destructive. "And where might that place be?" I added calmly.

"You don't need to know," she replied. "Traitor."

I bit at my lip, trying my hardest to suppress my anger. "Look, tell me where they are or there will be hell to pay. *Literally*."

Eva laughed. "And what exactly are you going to do? I know all about you, you can't control your power at all."

I narrowed my eyes. "You really want to test me and see for

yourself?" Though I had no faith in my words, I had to at least pretend to have some strength.

"Look, enough," Hunter suddenly spouted. "This is my fault, I shouldn't have taken her away like that, but I just panicked, please just let her see them."

Conner shrugged his shoulders. "We can't, don't know where they took them."

I clenched my fists even tighter. "You are kidding me?!"

"Look, we don't know, alright? We just follow orders. Anyhow, you have to stay here—Dr. Lincoln's orders."

They began to walk past me and head out the door, way too relaxed.

"You all really want to abide by their rules, even when they've brainwashed you like this?"

All their gazes turned to face me. "They haven't brainwashed us, Dr. Lincoln's facility helped us gain control of not only our powers but our lives. He gave us a helping hand when no one else would," said Adrian.

"It's all an illusion, right Hunter?"

Hunter bit at his lip, not knowing how to respond, as in reality his mind was still being powered by lies and he couldn't yet tell what was right or wrong. "Something is wrong in this situation, I can feel it. However, I can't tell what to believe right now. I just know Lexia is right in some way."

"See," I urged back, as they all thought over Hunter's words.

"Look, if you can't prove anything, I'm not going to believe a traitor like you, alright?" Eva said viciously.

Lucas' eyes suddenly gleamed. "I think she is telling the truth," he said, analysing my face.

"And how can you be so sure?" enquired Conner.

He shrugged his shoulders, digging his hands into his pockets. "I don't know, I just feel like she is."

"Oh, well, that sure is evidence. Come on, let's get out of here," Eva stated, but no one followed her and Lucas still kept his concentration on me.

"How did you find this all out, this supposed brainwashing?" Lucas said, for the first time he wasn't smirking at me and instead just looked with genuine interest.

I cleared my throat. "When I arrived, I sensed something was odd about this place. However, it wasn't till Hunter has made me see how you are all brainwashed—he was never like this before. Then when Hunter just transported me, we bumped into an old roommate and she was tied to a bed, getting injected by this killer liquid. She told us to leave or we will be next."

I could tell they were all processing my words through their tarnished minds—even Eva. Whether they would believe me or not depended on just how powerful that memory remover stuff was, but I couldn't worry about them, I had to find the others first and get out of here.

"I have to get out of here. I know you won't understand but please, just tell me where my friends are," I urged.

The group exchanged glances. "The guards took them away to the deport room." Lucas said.

She couldn't understand why he actually told her but didn't argue about it. But then again, Lucas was the only one who seemed willing as well. Like he was half on her side, but she did not know why. "What is that?"

"A place where they basically get rid of toxic waste - through gas," Lucas replied.

My eyes widened. "You mean they are going to gas them to death? Why?" I urged, the panic setting in even more.

"Because if Dr. Lincoln doesn't find someone useful, he gets rid of them. Often in harsh ways, depends how he feels," Conner added.

"Oh my God." I latched onto Hunters arm. "Can you teleport me there please? Do you know where it is?"

Hunter looked concerned. "I know where it is, I don't know if I can though, under all this pressure."

"Hunter, this is your damn brother's life at stake here, come on!" I yelled.

I could tell his old self was trying to rise through, as he closed his eyes and tried to focus his powers. He put out his hand, I placed my palm in it, and just before we were about to take off in the familiar whirlwind haze, Lucas spoke up.

"Lexia, be careful. Dr. Lincoln won't feel any guilt in killing you too. He may want you, but if you play him too much, he will destroy you." Lucas' words surprised me by how open he was being. But the other guys didn't seem so happy. I went over to Hunter and they could tell I was getting ready to leave now.

"Hey, where do you think you're going, you can't leave." Connor interjected.

"Try and stop us!" I shouted back, latching my hand through Hunter's arm, not even knowing if he would transport us before Connor grabbed me. Hunter thankfully managed to just get us away.

The last thing I saw was Lucas' smile and he gave a nod just as Hunter managed to transport us through a time tunnel, to where the fight for survival would truly begin.

Thirty-Two

We landed with a thud on the stone cold ground and as I rubbed my forehead and gazed at the new scenery surrounding us, I realized we had arrived in a place that was far different from the shining corridors of the usual facility. In fact, it looked like we weren't even in the same place anymore. Narrowing my eyes at the odd space, I looked towards Hunter, who seemed happy with himself for performing on cue.

"Are we in the right place? This doesn't even look like we are anywhere in the facility anymore," I enquired in confusion.

He nodded, his triumphant smile fading. "That is because we are underground. This part is locked off to most of us. I accidentally transported myself here a while back and when they said the deport room, I remembered the sign, so I knew this was the place."

I nodded as I gazed around. The halls were so dark down here, the walls painted a slate grey that matched the scuffed flooring. The walls were only lit by small yellow lights, hanging loosely from the ceiling.

"Now, it's time to find them," I said, trying to remove how eerie this place felt from my mind. "And the faster the better!"

We started trawling down the dimly lit corridors, checking each door as it came. However, as we came to the end of the hall, familiar voices suddenly came from the other end. Then I saw who it was: a guard carrying Xavier and Colt, who were seemingly knocked out. He walked into a room with Dr. Lincoln, before disappearing out of view.

As the door slammed shut, my fists angrily clenched together at the sight of those guys passed out. I now knew that if I had to, I would somehow use my power, hoping that I didn't kill my friends in the process. Whether I could control it or not was another matter—but I had to try.

I turned to face Hunter, who didn't look confident with the whole situation as we hid behind the wall to the entrance they were at. "So, I guess we are just going to have to storm the place. Do you think if worst came to worst, you could teleport us out of there?"

His eyes glistened, still looking unconfident. "This pressure, I can't handle it," he cried.

I let out a heavy sigh, just wishing the old, more confident Hunter would come back.

"Look, just try, okay?" I said, putting a comforting hand on his shoulder. "If we can't, then I guess we will have to die, but at least we tried. We have to at least make an effort to save them, especially after all Xavier has done for us. Even though he is a pain most of the time, we have to try." I curled my arms around Hunter's waist maybe for the last time. "We can do this," I muttered, trying not to tear up.

For a moment, Hunter just stood there stiff as a board, but suddenly his arms wrapped around my waist and he whispered, "Let's do this."

I felt a strange sense of familiarity and as I looked up into his eyes; they didn't seem as glazed over.

"Hunter?" I mouthed in shock at his sudden change in expression.

His gaze froze as he looked down at me, seemingly examining my face as his brain tried to work out who I was. Then suddenly something surprising happened—he lifted his head down to mine and our lips met.

My whole body froze with shock as he pressed his soft lips against mine. It was so unexpected that I didn't know what to do; I just stood there, wide-eyed and confused, wondering if he had been taken over by something again. However, as he pulled away, I saw his familiar relaxed expression come back on his face—the one that I had grown to love.

"What was that for?" I mouthed quietly, our eyes just gazing at each other awkwardly.

"I don't know. I just feel strange. I just knew I had to do that, just in case we never got to."

"*Bad* strange?"

"No, like a fog has been lifted off my brain and finally it would let me do that," he said simply.

"Do what? Kiss me? You have wanted to kiss me all this time, when I just thought we were friends?" I urged.

"Well, I know I've liked you, but couldn't do anything because of Xavier."

"You wanted to kiss me, before they wiped some of your memory?" I repeated.

His eyebrows raised. "They wiped some of my memory?"

I nodded back.

"So, that is why I couldn't vent my feelings. After I fell into the bout of depression, after we found we had to stay here longer, I felt angry at myself for being so cold to you when you were being so kind. I was going to confess to you and say sorry, just hoping you'd let me. I can't tell you how much I've wanted to do that, especially when I saw you after I'd killed Alvan. Though, that is all I seem to remember. What is going on? As soon as I kissed you, it was like I had woken from a dream."

I couldn't believe what he was saying. We had been close but over the past few weeks, I had been closer to Xavier than anybody and so this kiss—I didn't know what to think of it. In fact, I couldn't think of it right now, as Xavier suddenly crossed my mind again and the realisation that my friends could be dead started to spread through me.

"Oh my God, come on, we have to go get them."

"What, so it is true they really have taken them down…?" Hunter suddenly saw the sign to the deport room as we walked closer. "I thought I had been dreaming."

"Sadly, you aren't and your brother is in there right now, about to be gassed, so we better hurry."

"Wait, how did we get here, nobody knows of this place?"

"You teleported us here."

"So, that wasn't a dream either then?"

I shook my head. "Look, we'll talk about all of this later—including feelings–but right now, let's save your brother. Otherwise none of us will make it out of here."

Hunter latched onto my hand as we stood outside the door and as we peered through the small window to the inside, I saw the guards and Dr. Lincoln, put on gas masks, while Xavier and Colt still lay unconscious on the floor.

"I'll freaking kill them for touching my brother!" he yelled. He was about to try and break through the door, but I pulled him back in time.

"Hunter, stop, we need to think of how we are going to do this!" I urged.

Hunter put back his anger for a moment. "You could use your power to distract them; I could teleport them out of here and then come back for you?"

"Only problem there is, none of us have control over our power, so we can't guarantee that will work."

"Well, it's going to have to because either way, I'm not leaving my brother in there. If we die doing this, I would rather die trying."

I nodded. "I guess you are right. So, on the count of three, should we burst in and attack?"

Hunter nodded and after one final hug, we counted to three and burst through the door, which was luckily unlocked. As we did so, everyone stared up at us in shock.

"Hand them over, you old fool!" shouted Hunter.

Dr. Lincoln laughed through his mask, while motioning for a man to press a button on a control. "You press that and I will blow up this room," I urged, placing out my hands and feeling the heat in my veins start to radiate.

I motioned for Hunter to move towards Xavier and Colt and get ready to transport them out of here, while I kept their concentration. Dr. Lincoln still motioned for the guard to press the button, and once he did, a fine gas started to pour into the room.

"Now!" I shouted to Hunter, while I pushed Dr. Lincoln, who went tumbling to the ground. Then I grabbed the remote from the guard, crushing it on the floor, hoping it would stop the gas—but it didn't.

As I turned to Hunter, he put both his hands over Xavier and Colt, closed his eyes and disappeared out of the room. I sighed in relief for a moment, until I saw the gas start to form around me and it began to clog up my lungs.

Suddenly I felt a hand latch onto my hair and Dr. Lincoln pulled me back, holding an injection in his hand, ready to stab it into my skin. However, before I could stop him or see what even happened, the gas fogged up my mind and I passed out, leaving my life in danger.

Thirty-Three

The gas still lingered in my mind for a moment, as I slowly started to return to reality; I just hoped the reality that was emerging through the fog wasn't one of me being a brainwashed zombie. After all, the last thing I saw was Dr. Lincoln holding that injection. As my senses started to clear, I suddenly heard a voice call my name and felt a hand caressing my cheek as I lay on the ground.

As my vision eventually cleared, I saw Xavier looking down at me with a tear-filled gaze and at first, I couldn't seem to believe it was him.

"Lexia," he mumbled through his tears, trying to wipe them away as he stroked my cheek.

"Xavier...?" I muttered back. "You're alright....?"

He let out a shaky laugh under his breath. "Don't worry about me, are you okay?"

Suddenly Hunter's voice raised beside me. "Is she alright?" he urged.

"I'm fine, just feel a bit foggy," I replied and slowly sat up, both of them sliding a hand around my waist to help me.

"I can't believe you let this happen Hunter, she could have died! Why did you teleport us out first and not her!" said Xavier through gritted teeth.

"Don't blame me!" replied hunter, holding his hands up in defence. "I was brainwashed, remember? Besides, it was the only way for us to get you guys out of there."

"He is right Xavier, he'd just broke out of it and he had to get you out then," I replied.

"How did you break out of it then?" asked Xavier.

As I looked towards Hunter for a moment, he didn't seem to

remember, until his eyes turned to me and widened, recalling the kiss he had planted on me. His face suddenly beaming red.

"What's wrong with you?" said Xavier, confused by his now ever-reddening cheeks.

"Uh, nothing, I just—" He froze, knowing that Xavier would hate him if he found out he had kissed me.

I broke into the conversation before it could escalate. "He just switched out of it when I told him he had to save you. It was like a light switch went on, you know?" I replied, nodding my head towards Hunter, who nodded back in agreement.

"Thanks, bro. I knew I could count on you, whether you were psycho or not," Xavier said, relieved.

To change the conversation, I quickly diverted it onto our surroundings. "Where am I?" I urged, staring out into a dying green field that was surrounded by rusting fences and nothing in sight for miles.

"Outside the facility. I managed to bring you here in time before that crazy arsehole stabbed you with whatever solution was in that needle," said Hunter.

"You did it then," I said, pleased for him yet surprised he'd done it so quick. "You were able to focus on your power." I smiled.

"Thanks to you," he said, returning the happiness. "You made me believe in myself."

I swallowed nervously as he said that, as I could tell it was getting back into the awkward zone. "No, that was all you—all you had to do was focus and you did. I just wish I could do the same."

I suddenly felt Xavier getting agitated by our talk and as he spoke up, he changed the conversation. "So, now we are all okay, what are we going to do?"

"Get out of here, I imagine," said Colt, suddenly appearing and giving me a wave, mouthing a *thank you* as he did so.

"I suppose..." I muttered, suddenly remembering about Elisa and the fact the other group members were still there.

"What about the others?" I urged.

"What about them?" spat Xavier.

"Well, shouldn't we help them too? I mean, they are there unwillingly and were brainwashed like Hunter. He has come out of it and maybe if we get them out of there, they will too."

Xavier's lip crooked up. "That isn't our problem—we are out of that hell hole now, I and ain't going back."

I turned my head back to Hunter, not appreciating Xavier's way of thinking. "Should we just leave them?" I urged.

Hunter bit at his lip for a moment, contemplating what to do. It surprised me that he didn't automatically agree with his brother; this was a rare occasion indeed.

"I suppose I could try and get them ... it's just that if we do, there is a risk of us dying this time around. Also, what if they don't want to come? It could be a waste of time and since we just got out, is it worth the risk?" He did hold a point. Since the others in the unit were brainwashed, would they even listen to her as only Lucas had shown any care when she had told them about everything. Was it a chance she was willing to take to save these guys who would probably kill her this time around. They may not even care if they are brainwashed and wouldn't be able to break out of it as easy as Hunter had because they had most likely been brainwashed so long now. But still, it felt wrong to just leave them without trying.

"Hell no," stated Xavier bluntly.

"Look, we have to at least save Elisa. She is a part of our group, we can't just leave her there to become one of them."

"Elisa?" spouted Colt. "She is still there; didn't she leave ages ago?"

I shook my head. "No. Hunter and I bumped into her while trying to save you two and she said they were slowly killing her and that we had to get out."

"Oh my God, we have to go and get her!" said Colt, jumping up.

"We just got out, there is no way I am going back! Besides, she always used to mock you, let her die." yelled Xavier.

"Shut up! She is a part of our group, we can't just abandon her!" Colt cried.

"A part of our group? We haven't seen her in weeks, so that hardly makes her 'one of our group' anymore. Anyhow, if you want to do it then you stay—have fun." Xavier replied, tapping Colt on the shoulder as he walked past.

I could see Colt's face burn with emotion and I knew he wouldn't be able to leave, knowing she was still here and they were treating her this way. I didn't even like her, but we couldn't leave her to rot away like this.

"We can't just leave her Xavier. Not like this," I urged, slowly shaking away his hand from mine as I stumbled up to my feet. I couldn't help wondering why I cared so much about others.

Xavier gazed down at me, not wanting to, but I could tell he couldn't say no to me. "So, what exactly is your plan then?" he said through gritted teeth.

My eyes turned to Hunter, who knew exactly what I was about to ask.

"Feel like teleporting again?" I smiled.

"I don't have much choice, do I?" Hunter replied, getting up and brushing away the dirt.

And so, we all stood in a circle together and Hunter teleported us back into the place.

Thirty-Four

Hunter managed to teleport us back into the facility, which I wasn't happy to see again. However, I couldn't leave Elisa to die and although it was contradictory for me to save a girl who annoyed me so much, when I didn't care I had killed my college bullies, I just had to do so. I had never had the chance to save someone before—whether at college or during my childhood incident—and now I had the opportunity.

"Where we going then?" Xavier asked through a frustrated sigh, as we started gazing down the halls and I tried to remember where it was I had last seen Elisa.

"She was in a room off the facility," I said.

Everyone followed me to the place Hunter had first taken me; scrambling through the halls as fast as we could to avoid the psychos that resided here.

I found it pretty easily. However, as we went inside, she was nowhere to be seen; the only thing there was the empty drip bag she had been attached to.

"Bloody hell, she isn't here!" I groaned, looking down the now empty stretch of beds.

"Oh great..." said Xavier, rolling his eyes. "How unexpected."

"Shut up, misery. She can't be far," I stated.

"Any clue where she may be then?" Hunter enquired.

I bit at my lip, trying to come up with where she could be, then realised the most likely place was outside of here.

"I have a feeling where she will be, follow me," I said. I had a feeling she had been taken to the unit where the rest of the brainwashed bunch lived. Once she was there, they would finally kill her to get back at us, as they must have seen Hunter and me talking to her on the cameras.

We ran through the halls again and Xavier used his power to blow away everyone who dared try to stop us, sending a bolt of electricity their way—which I think he enjoyed. We stopped outside the double doors to the facility and looked inside to see the group: Dr. Lincoln and the guards were all standing around Elisa as she stood in the middle of them.

"There she is," croaked Colt, as he got ready to run inside.

"Colt, wait! We need to plan this! Just because they didn't attack us last time doesn't mean they won't now."

However, Xavier pushed past me with a poker face and entered the room nonchalantly, his hand tucked in his pockets as he ignored my words.

"Xavier!" I yelled, all eyes lay on him.

We had no choice but to follow him in, Hunter ready to teleport us all at any given moment.

"Hey, you old fool, look who's back," he spouted to Dr. Lincoln, who gazed at Xavier with surprise. "Time for some payback. You tried to kill me, so time I repaid the favour, eh."

Dr. Lincoln's gaze soon smoothed and he just stood there with a smirk, as he motioned towards Adrian to attack him. Adrian obeyed and just as he was about to attack, Xavier shot up his hand without looking and a gush of blue light exploded from his palm, sending Adrian flying to the ground.

Everyone looked around in shock and the smirk was now wiped off Dr. Lincoln's face. He put his hands up in defence: "Look, now, Xavier, we can talk about this. I'll give you a job here with all the money you could desire—as a way to say I'm sorry."

"How tempting," Xavier joked, striding casually closer to him.

Dr. Lincoln motioned towards the rest of the group to attack, but none of them listened, not wanting to respond to what they just seen.

"Good idea," Xavier smiled, while going to stand in front of Dr. Lincoln, who looked petrified now.

While Xavier distracted him, I turned my attention toward Elisa and the rest of the group. "Guys, come with us and get out of here! There is nothing for you here." They all took a glance towards each other but to no surprise, they just shook their heads. I let out a sigh as I gazed to Lucas, who gave a half smile, but shook his head too. I just had a feeling they were letting us leave. Why, I didn't know. However, I soon had to let the feeling go as Colt ran to Elisa and dragged her over to us, her weak body limping alongside him. I was surprised to see she was still alive. Adrian was just about to get up and hit them, but Lucas pulled him back.

"*Go,*" he muttered under his breath as he held Adrian back.

I said *Thank You* back, still feeling sad I hadn't gotten to know him more. However, I soon shook the others away, as I turned my attention back towards Dr. Lincoln and Xavier. "Xavier, let's get out of here."

Just when I thought he was about to send a bolt to hit Dr. Lincoln, Hunter put a hand on Xavier's shoulders and told him it wasn't worth it. So instead, he just punched him and returned to us.

"Let's get out of here," stated Hunter.

Xavier sent a glare towards Dr. Lincoln, who flinched as he watched him lay his hands back down by his sides. "You are lucky today, you old fool. All of you are. But if I ever see or hear you again, you'll feel more than my blue bolt radiating up your arse."

As Hunter dragged moody Xavier away, Xavier came and wrapped me into a hug, as we all formed a circle and felt the familiar wind tunnel transport us outside, me taking one last glimpse at Lucas, who gave a small wave and smirk before we disappeared.

However, as we landed outside, I wasn't automatically filled with relief. I just had a feeling that this wouldn't be the end. I knew we would forever be hunted now by these people and so, I couldn't just leave this place standing. I had to destroy it and that meant only one thing: using my power to blow up this building and me with it.

Thirty-Five

As we started walking out of the gated fence that Xavier had broken through, a mound of nothing but desolation surrounding us as we did so, I saw everybody looking content with the fact we were finally free.

Colt and Elisa were oddly holding hands as he steadied her along, and it was good to see Xavier and Hunter back to their close old ways that I had missed so much. However, I couldn't feel good. I still hadn't gained control of my ability—leaving me open to becoming like my dad and meaning my aunt would be left disappointed. We were leaving here and that would mean we were criminals, as nobody would believe us about what had truly happened behind the scenes, given the reasons we were all here in the first place. Dr. Lincoln was bound to alert the supernatural jail and if we were caught, we would be sent there, because we wouldn't be allowed to leave until they had signed for us to do so.

Even though it all left a bitter taste as I turned back around to face the facility that stood so grimly before me, I knew what I had to do. I had to destroy this place or we would forever have these people on our backs. But I mainly had to destroy it because I knew they would continue to prey on vulnerable supernaturals time and time again, brainwashing them into thinking they were even more useless than they already thought, turning them into zombies for their own gain.

As everyone passed through to the other side of the gates, I knew what I had to do. Although I knew we would become fugitives and there would be more places like this in the world, I just had to destroy it. I didn't want other supernaturals to have to face this.

As the others stepped outside the gates, I waited till everyone had gone a slight distance ahead of me before I grabbed the lock Xavier had burned off and quickly melted the gate back shut with it, using what power I could conjure up. The clanking of the metal frame bashing together made everyone turn in shock and seeing me stand on the other end, they were all riddled with confusion.

"What's going on?" Xavier said walking over to me, looking confused as to why I was so upset and why I had locked myself inside.

"I have to stay," I replied, as calm as I could.

Xavier let out a laugh. "What are you talking about? Come on." He came back to the fence, ready to open the gate again, but I burned his hands away.

"I have to destroy the place, stay back," I stated, feeling the flames I could control tickle at my palms as I watched him flinch back.

Xavier's expression soon simmered as he glanced at his scorched hands with surprise. "What the heck! Come on Lexia, let's go already!" He pouted, just about to break through the gate as I saw the electric blue rays begin to trickle through his arms.

"Xavier, stop—or I'll make you!" I said, my hands glowing red.

He didn't listen and continued to try and break back through, so I had no choice but to ignite the gate post, which I couldn't believe I actually managed to do, given I could only usually produce small flames. However, I knew it was the anger and frustration inside of me helping to fuel it, knowing that this had to be done and I was the only one capable of destroying this place.

"What the heck!" he yelled again, getting back up and trying to break through the flames, but they just kept glowing vividly in front of him.

"Let me in here, Lexia. We're leaving!" I could see he was trying to hold back his sadness, but I had to do this in order to keep them away. Keep other vulnerable supernaturals safe.

"Why do you have to stay here?" said Hunter with gleaming eyes, as I just managed to gaze at him through the fiery blaze.

"Because If I don't destroy this place, then other supernatural youth will go through this too. And I can't have that. Besides, these people deserve to die," I stated back.

"I understand why you would want to, but this isn't the only facility like this; there are still going to be so many other places like it," Hunter exclaimed and I almost wanted to kiss him through the orange fence, as I saw him trying to hold back a tear, which soon floated away as the anger mounted.

I nodded. "I know, but destroying one is better than nothing."

Xavier let out a frustrated sigh. "Seriously, Lexia, let me in or I will force myself through. Fire or no fire. I don't understand why you care about helping others by destroying this place, you have killed people yourself."

Xavier's words stung, as I knew I had killed. However, that didn't mean I couldn't help people either—people like me. "I have to do this, Xavier, or else there will be no end to this. I know I have killed, but at least if I destroy this place then it's a step in the right direction. I'm saving future people."

"Then I'm going with you. I won't let it end this way!" he shouted as I began to step back towards the facility.

"You can't. You have to stay alive to fight these people, you are too strong to die," I urged, trying not to let my tears get in the way. Even Colt and Elisa started telling me to stop from behind them.

"We seriously have to go now if we want to get away, who knows if my power will work for us all." Hunter said.

"Go, please, Xavier. You have to fight this establishment. Save other people like ourselves and help them to get proper help."

He looked down at me with glistening eyes. "Lexia, I can't just let you go and do this," he said in a soft voice.

"Well, you have no choice," I muttered, making the flames burn even higher and brighter now so I could no longer see them, my determination and anger fuelling the height of the fire. "I have to do this. I'm sorry."

"Seriously, Lexia, let me back in now or I will force my way back!" Xavier cried even louder.

"Then I will just have to throw you back out again. Leave now. You have to be away from this space when I blow it up, as it won't be pretty."

As a tear ran down my cheek, I quickly turned and was about to head to the building, sad that this may be the way that Xavier and I ended. However, I had to exit this way, not only because my anger was now taking me over, but also because it was too hard to look at their faces any longer. However, as I tried to rid them from my mind, Hunter teleported in front of me, blocking the way. He rested his hands on my shoulders and as our eyes met, I tried to hold back my tears. "You don't have to do this, we can destroy this place together, this isn't the only option."

"But, it is, Hunter. I have to do this, these people have lied not only to us, but to the world. Even if this doesn't amount to anything in the future, I have to get them back, one way or another. My anger won't allow me to hold back; if I don't let out this blast now, it will just mount up and I will have another incident like the college one. I have to do this."

For a moment, he just stared down at me and for a second, I thought our lips were going to meet again. Instead, he just threw me into a hug and whispered *'Be safe'* into my ear, before letting me go and teleporting back to the other side.

"Why didn't you bring her back, damn it!" Xavier yelled.

"We have to go, Xavier," Hunter replied and I faintly saw him dragging them away.

"Shut up! I'm not leaving. Lexia, please just come here..."

I so badly wanted to reach for his hand and just rest in his arms. But I couldn't. Even though there were more of these places, I couldn't miss the opportunity of destroying this one; I didn't want anyone else being sent here to face the lies and abuse. Nobody deserved it and if I could just save a few people by destroying this place, then I would be happy.

The tears began to stream down my cheeks, but I couldn't look behind and as I headed to the entrance door, he began screaming my name. I froze a moment at the door before closing it and hiding away from his voice for what could be forever.

I had to act this quickly and coldly, or his words would tempt me, and I couldn't let them. When people hurt me, I had to hurt them back and let out the building anger with my power, as it was my outlet. Months of emotions had built up inside me and now I had to release them. It was time for action. I wiped away my tears and buried their faces to the back of my mind, hoping that Hunter got everyone out in time before this place blew up.

I was headed to the centre base, where the main headquarters was. Once I got there, it was goodbye to everything in sight—me included.

My whole body trembled, but I had a mission to complete and even though I was sacrificing my life, something of which I thought I had always been too selfish to do, it had to be done. This place was decayed and needed removing, and I was the only one who could successfully do that; come live or die.

I stormed through the corridors before they even had a chance to capture me, destroying all the cameras and killing everyone who was in my way as my emotions started to numb, before finally I got to the main base. As I looked inside, everyone was panicking as they sat at their desks and looked at the large screens, trying to figure out what was happening as fire began to consume the halls. Well, they would soon find out. I took a deep breath and as I pushed open the door, all eyes turned to me. Everyone seemed to freeze at my presence and as I went and stood in the centre of the room.

People began looking around at each other frantically, not knowing how to tackle a supernatural being, as these were the people working behind the scenes, never actually having to deal with the supernaturals at hand. I felt my pulse and heartbeat racing like they had never before and I had only one mission in mind now: to destroy these people who had dared fault the supernatural kind.

"It's her!" Someone yelled and as I turned my head, I saw Dr. Lincoln looking at me with concern. I could see he didn't know how to respond as I walked over to him, just freezing in place as he had been watching me from the security cameras of which most were now blacked-out. My gaze drifted towards them: the screens held a view of every place I had stayed in or been, they had been watching us closely the entire time and had used Ben as their ears to report what we had talked about.

I saw my friends standing outside the fence, Hunter finally dragging Xavier away, who was clinging on to the ground. A tear couldn't help but form at my eyes, as even though I had survived creating a blast before—when Ben had attacked me and of course, my disastrous college incident and childhood chaos—I didn't know whether my body could handle it this time. After all, I wasn't just going to let out a tiny part of my power this time; this would be strong enough to destroy the whole building. I would be amazed if I survived, as this was one huge facility.

I swallowed my nerves and let a grin curl at my lips as I gazed towards Dr. Lincoln again, Ben standing uncharacteristically quietly by his side. For a moment, the brainwashed unit entered my mind and I felt sad that they were going to have to die. However, there was nothing I could do, as they did not want to leave.

"Lexia, we will give you one last chance. Stay here and we will give you whatever you desire, because if you don't, you will just become criminals like them," Dr. Lincoln urged, pointing over to the screen showing my friends, who were now teleporting away, which made me sigh internally with relief.

I laughed. "I'm already a criminal, you old fool."

And as I lifted both my hands in the air, I could see he was beginning to panic and knew what was coming.

"Lexia, stop this!" he yelled.

But I started to blur him and everyone else out. Thinking of all the things they had done to us, to make my anger boil and thus make the explosion worse. My power stormed through my body as there was so much I hated this place for. The lies. The spying. The torture. All of it. I couldn't leave here knowing it still existed, so even if this destruction of this place only made one difference, then I would be happy.

"Goodbye, idiots. Remember never to mess with supernatural beings again."

And as my power got to its full capacity, I felt my whole body start to burn from the heat, my veins now beaming with an orange tinge which meant it was ready to blow.

It was sad to see that I had to do this again. *Kill.* However, I had to do this and even though I had not learnt to control my ability, I could say I had accomplished one goal—I was not my father. I was persevering and even though this blast could kill me—just like he took his own life—I would never compare myself to that man again. Therefore, if I did die now, I didn't care. I was dying to save people. Vulnerable people. Something I had not done before and something that he did not die for. He died without saying goodbye. Without apologising for hurting me and my mother. Without helping to tame the beast in my soul that he had too. And even though I was not a perfect person and you could rank me as a murderer—unlike him, I knew my faults. And now, I was going to use my fault to save people like me from ever having to come here.

The air started to whip around me and as it picked up, papers and computers started to crash everywhere as the heat filled the room, and I heard faint yells from everybody. But it was too late, my power was here and as I opened my eyes to stare at the person responsible, I couldn't help but smirk for one last time. Just before my power blew everything into a fiery blaze around me and my mind fluttered into darkness.

Thirty-Six

I gasped for air as I felt the dust particles settle around me, my eyes unable to open for a few moments as I could only focus on the smoke choking my throat. As I felt the dust calm around me, and the chilly breeze brushed by my bare arms, my eyes slowly managed to open and the sight that revealed itself around me was of nothing but a hazed out grave of destruction.

Everything lay in rubble and wreckage around me; dust and smoke lingering in the air around what looked like a blown-up building I was lying inside. Bricks and dirt lay scattered by my battered body, which soon made me look down at my arms more intently; they were covered in dirt, bruises and scratches and the more I moved, the more pain I felt. And, of course, the memorable burned-out orange colour that only arose when I used my power stained my veins. I also felt a throbbing pain in my hands, which hurt the most. As I looked down, I saw that the palms of my hands were red raw too, and covered in burn marks. As I observed my veins closer, I noted how singed with deep red burns they were; even worse than when I had lost control at college because now you could practically see right through my skin

I looked up from my wounds and back to the scene, to a small pit of fire that lay on one side of the destroyed building. Broken bricks and burnt out spaces lay where the facility had once stood. All I could do was sit there, in the chaos, confused as to what had happened.

That was until I heard Xavier's voice calling me and the images of everything started to float back slowly.

My anger. The betrayal. The goodbyes. All of it came pouring back and oddly, I was not automatically greeted by an overwhelming sense of frustration that I had lost control again. In fact, it was quite the opposite. I felt content. Something that had never happened before, after I had used my ability. Because I knew that for once, I had used it for a reason and not just a release.

I took a deep breath and slowly pulled myself up, as I was guided to Xavier's calls, nearly tumbling all over the rubble as I did so. The pain making me almost fall back down. However, I managed to steady myself and followed his familiar tone.

As I heard Xavier's voice getting closer, I used up all my energy to trek through the wreckage, until I came upon a clear stretch of path that looked out upon a huge view of the decayed fields. As I gazed deeper into the shroud, squinting my eyes in the process, I noticed two tall figures standing in the shadows and I suddenly heard a voice break through the smoke.

"Lexi!" Xavier yelled, suddenly climbing through the wreckage towards me as I kept walking.

"Lexia..." Xavier and Hunter both murmured a little lower this time, as we got to each other and before I knew it, I was wrapped in both their arms, tears bleeding down my cheeks. I had now even forgotten how much pain I was in, as I was just glad I had survived and that I was in their arms again.

After a few moments of not wanting to let each other go, they pulled back and Xavier held my face and smiled with a teary gaze, his face stained with the smoke, my eyes shifting between him and Hunter, as he stood there awkwardly, remembering Xavier didn't know he had kissed me.

"Don't ever do that again, okay?" Xavier cried, hugging me even tighter. Hunter just stood in the background, forcing a smile and digging his hands into his tattered black jeans.

I turned my gaze away from him and snuggled into Xavier's neck, as the weird stuff happening between us was the least of my worries right now.

"I'm sorry, I had to," I mumbled. "Once my anger takes over, that's it—no one can stop me. Only thing is though, I've killed more people, it's horrible." I was most upset that I had probably killed Lucas more than anyone, because I would have loved to have gotten to know a fellow pyrokinetic more.

"People that were going to kill us, Lexia," interjected Hunter. "You did the right thing. If I had your power, I would have done the same. These people wouldn't have stopped, they would have continued to take vulnerable supernaturals again and again, and you just put an end to their tirade. And even though I assume there will be other places like this, at least you have destroyed one of them, meaning no other kid will have to go through what we did."

"I'm just glad you're okay, I was about to kill Hunter myself for letting you go if you weren't."

"I knew she would be fine. You think I would have let her go otherwise?" grumbled Hunter.

"You think that's fine?" he gestured at the state of me, and the blood that covered me.

"It's nothing compared to me saving other people from this place. These liars," I shot back.

"Anyhow, we better go, because I have a feeling that not everyone will have died as we weren't the only ones with powers in there. Come on," Hunter said as he put out his hand to us.

I placed my hand in his palm instantly, just wanting to leave this horrid life behind. "Where exactly are we going to go?"

"We'll find somewhere," Xavier smiled, as he placed his palm in Hunter's and his grip tightened around mine. Hunter then closed his eyes and we were taken away, leaving the place that should've been my saving grace behind.

Even though I was sad it had failed and that I had to kill again, I wasn't completely unhappy. Not only had I learned how truly strong I was, but I had actually met a cool group of people—something that I wouldn't admit to their faces of course, but I truly did like them. I also had learned that I wasn't my father; I wasn't horrid and weak like him. Because unlike the man who gave me this destructive ability and raised me in a terrible way, I could learn from my mistakes and I wanted to grow. And that thought was enough to get me through the hell that lay ahead.

We knew that just because this place was destroyed, it didn't mean the adventure was over yet. And neither was the fact we still couldn't control our abilities. However, I would teach myself. As unlike my father, I knew life was too precious not to try and live and add some light back into the darkness we had created.

THE END